The making of VIRGIN.. MIRA

first Guerrilla Feature-Film from the APAC

Book 2 by Lord Baden-Powell
National Award winning filmmaker

Amit R Agarwal

Published By

Redgrab Books Pvt. Ltd.

942, Mutthiganj, Prayagraj, 211003

www.redgrabbooks.com

contact@redgrabbooks.com

Price in india :225/- INR

First published by Redgrab Books in 2023

Printed and bound in India

Cover Design & Typesetting by Redgrab Books team

ISBN : 978-93-95697-23-1

ABOUT THE BOOK

'The Making of Virgin.. Mira' is the second book written by yours truly

- Amit R Agarwal

The fact that my mother has written the foreword for this book makes 'The Making of Virgin.. Mira' the most important book in my life; also the most important artistic and creative work for me!

Interestingly, Book 1 "Cine माँ, Success के लिए Act Now" compiled from the e-book and various blogs I had written on my website talked about माँ and how a film-maker just can't make a blockbuster without माँ

This book is based on the film I made, Virgin.. Mira, specifically for the international market

I still remember that when I made Virgin.. Mira in 2006, 2007 and 2008, a few people said that it might hurt a few sentiments.

I questioned, how?

Mira is a universal name.

Ironically we have two very popular actresses,

Mira Sorvino and Meera, both are non-Hindus.

The beauty of Hindusism is that it is universal and finds an echo across the world.

That is the richness of our culture and ethos

Hinduism was way ahead of its times, imagine our ancestors of yore

wrote Kamasutra when world was still reeling under ignorance and lack of education

Coming to Virgin.. Mira the film is about Mira Ali. She wants to realize her father's dream of studying and wiping off the infamy her brother brought to their family. Alone in the big bad world, she decides to auction her virginity. The man who bids for her virginity is a lonely man, Raghav Krishna.

The film is about the beautiful bond between two scarred souls

The book is about how I made the first guerrilla feature-film in the APAC region

प्रस्तावना

प्रिय पुत्र,

कला एवं सृजनता का क्षेत्र अत्यंत विषमताओं एवं कठिनाईयों भरा है, पर फिर भी हर युग में कलाकार एवं सृजनकर्ता जन्में हैं और उनकी कला आज भी अमर है।

आज के युग में लोग उस युग के नगर सेठों को भले ही भूल गए हों लेकिन कलाकार आज भी याद हैं ।

साहित्य की बात हो रही है तो, मुंशी प्रेमचंद और सादत हसन मंटो ने अपने जीवन काल में अत्यंत विषमताओं को झेला, पर आज के युग में वो कई कलाकारों की प्रेरणा का स्रोत हैं।

मुझे याद है जब तुमने मुझे 'वर्जिन मीरा' फिल्म के बारे में बताया था तो एक पल को मैं स्तब्ध रह गयी थी, पर जिस बारीकी से तुमने अपनी फिल्म पर काम किया था, उससे मुझे खुद पर गर्व हुआ था की कला और सृजनता में तुम अपनी पीढ़ी के अग्रणी हो।

निसंदेह नारी के लिए आज पूरी दुनिया में आंदोलन हो रहे हैं और तुम्हारी फिल्म भी नारी के आत्म-सम्मान एवं उसकी सुरक्षा की बात करती है।

मुझे पूरी उम्मीद है की तुम्हारी पुस्तक, कला और सृजनता के क्षेत्र में काम कर रहे और आने वाले वर्षों में काम करने आ रहे लोगों के लिए एक प्रेरणा-स्रोत होगी।

अनेक अनेक आशीर्वाद एवं सुभाशीष के साथ,

तुम्हारी माँ

CONTENT

PHOTO GALLERY

City director on silver screen debut

VIRGINITY FOR SALE

बहरीन से आई 'मीरा'

वर्जिनिटी कोई सस्ती चीज नहीं

रीमा अली

Chapter 1

Chapter 2A

Chapter 2B -1

Chapter 2B -2

Chapter 3

Chapter 4A

Chapter 4B

Chapter 5A

Chapter 5B

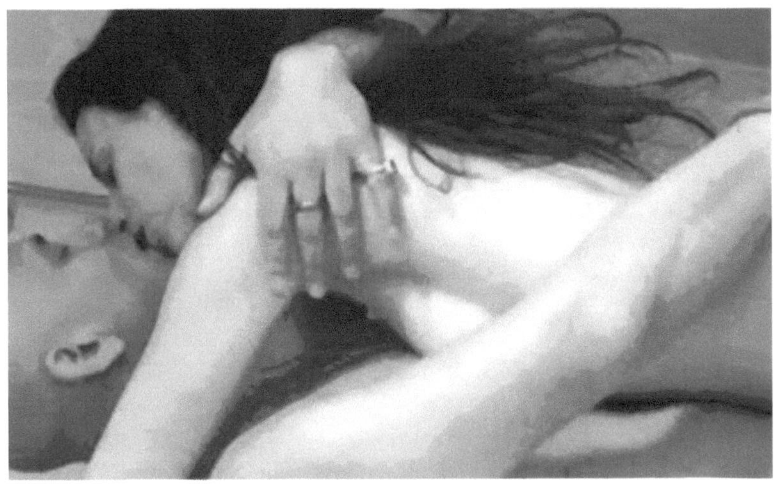

Chapter 6A

Chapter 6B

Chapter 7

Chapter 8A

Chapter 8B

Chapter 9A

Chapter 9B

Chapter 10

Chapter 11

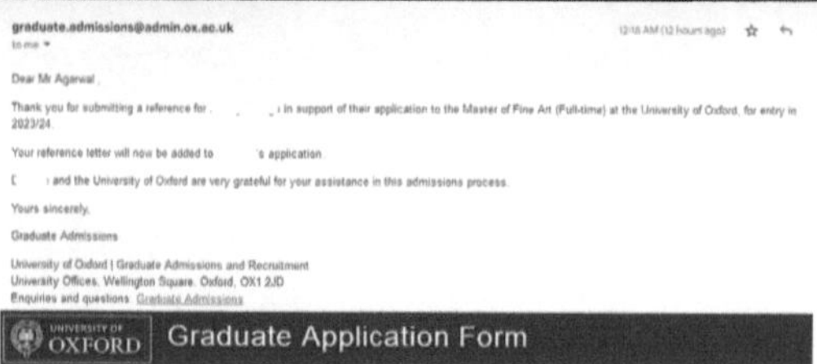

graduate.admissions@admin.ox.ac.uk
to me

12:18 AM (12 hours ago)

Dear Mr Agarwal ,

Thank you for submitting a reference for , in support of their application to the Master of Fine Art (Full-time) at the University of Oxford, for entry in 2023/24.

Your reference letter will now be added to 's application.

and the University of Oxford are very grateful for your assistance in this admissions process.

Yours sincerely,

Graduate Admissions

University of Oxford | Graduate Admissions and Recruitment
University Offices, Wellington Square, Oxford, OX1 2JD
Enquiries and questions: Graduate Admissions

UNIVERSITY OF OXFORD Graduate Application Form

Reference Submitted

Your reference has been submitted.

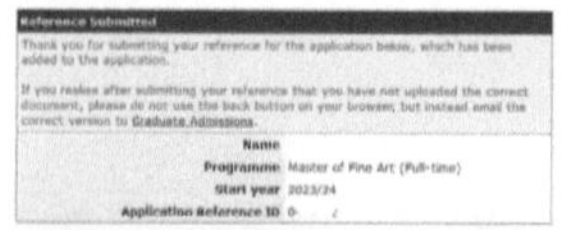

Reference Submitted

Thank you for submitting your reference for the application below, which has been added to the application.

If you realise after submitting your reference that you have not uploaded the correct document, please do not use the back button on your browser, but instead email the correct version to Graduate Admissions.

Name	
Programme	Master of Fine Art (Full-time)
Start year	2023/24
Application Reference ID	0-

Epilogue

Chapter – 1
THE 9-MONTH RULE

first things first.

The language of this book, like my previous book, Cine माँ which was based on my blog and e-book available on https://www.popcornflicks.org is hugely abstract. This is because experimental is not the right word to use in literature.

The chapters are consciously and intentionally disjointed because like the previous book I am treating writing this book more of a memoir – a collage of experiences that shaped the first guerrilla feature-film of the APAC region, Virgin.. Mira.

The line underneath is repetitive, but I use it in all my MasterClasses, so here it is!

Let me wish each and every reader, in any part of the world, cutting across caste, creed, sex, nationality, race, religion – All The Very Best – to shine as a successful film-professional. I am sure after reading this book, your journey in the film, entertainment and media industry will be a lot easier.

This book is about how I went on to make the first guerrilla feature film of APAC with practically no money at all or should I say because I had no money, I had to make the film guerrilla-style!

City director on silver screen debut

VIRGINITY FOR SALE

वर्जिनिटी कोई सस्ती चीज नहीं

रीमा अली

बहरीन से आई मीरा

In my previous book, I talked about the 9-month rule.

Having spent 9-months in the industry, I pitched the idea of Virgin.. Mira to a National Award-winning producer. His father was a famous film producer as well, having produced a blockbuster with none other than the magician of the box-office and one of my fav filmmakers, Manmohan Desai.

After being kept on the hook for, ironically 9-months, I realized this scum of a producer wanted to set the film in London, without me involved in the film or me getting paid for the idea, story and screenplay.

My first lesson about the dirty producers, Bollywood is infamous for.

I have always been very upfront about things. I told him in his Arabian-sea facing flat in Versova that I am already planning to shoot the film. Mind you, without even knowing if I will be able to do even a days' shoot.

I remember his look very clearly, he was like; have you really found a producer?

Without a producer in tow, I bluffed, 'yes'. The bluff was necessary.

He was like, "ok you make your own; I will make mine with a new title".

Mine. That was a really big statement.

The sheer audacity with which he was ready to steal, the fact that the script was registered with Screen Writers' Association or the title was registered with a film producers' association didn't budge him.

No wonder even after 16 years, he is yet to announce a film.

Chapter – 2A

CINEMA, MY FIRST LESSON

This abuse of power, this blatant use of contacts was my first lesson in the industry, as I had already mentioned in Chapter 1.

This first lesson about the dirty producers, Bollywood is infamous for, put me off the producers such that I stopped pitching to studios or producers after this incident.

Of course after almost a decade and a half two of my scripts, Beauty and The Baldie and Beehad Bhediya that I pitched to studios and producers got out, proving my worst fears.

After this brutal harsh reality of the film industry, I was wondering what to do with the film. How to make the film?

During this time I got to know about Guerilla Films.

Guerrilla films are; as-is-where-is-style shot films that need a very strong script to work. I knew I had a great story and a very strong script (for the year 2006).

I knew Virgin.. Mira was just the right film to kickstart my filmmaking career, but Guerrilla Films, I was perplexed.

Before I detail it, here is a chapter on Guerrilla Filmmaking from my filmmaking blog that of course you know became my first book, Cine माँ

Chapter – 3
GUERRILLA FILMMAKING

When I started making Guerrilla Films, it was tough to explain to people – the cast and the crew, what guerrilla films are.

The as-is-where-is-style shot films that are driven by very strong script, wasn't the kind of cinema a majority of novices knew.

Everyone wanted a bollywood-style debut, but how many really get a bollywood-styled debut? 1% of all aspirants; may be 3%. Any figure above that is a fallacy!

Thanks to the immense media frenzy; everyone knows about Cannes Film Festival, but how many know about Palme d'Or. I am not just talking about Indians, but aspiring cast and crew across the world.

Talking about guerrilla-films, few Indian actors brought to fore the hypocrisy, we the Asians are infamous for. Of course, in the following years, I found hypocrisy is a universal trait, less in the west, but very much there!

I cast westerners in full fledged roles, speaking Hindi; grooving and moving on to bollywood songs. Again, a radically innovative way of filmmaking but one that I knew will fit well in my narrative, gel well in the script.

A fact corroborated by the casting of the lead actress in Virgin.. Mira. After auditioning more than 100-actresses, I zeroed in on a girl raised in Bahrain, Reema Ali.

Her dedication and her no-nonsense attitude towards work absolutely floored me and I cast her for the titular role of Mira Ali.

I found her to be quite the opposite of many Indian actresses that frequent the auditions.

I feel it's all about the exposure you have in the world and how well-read a person you are. For example a few Indian actresses that audition often ask me "Are there any bold scenes?"

I am like "excuse me, what do you mean by bold?"

If you mean sex and nudity; call them sex scenes or nude scenes or love-making scenes. Using 'bold' is a very shady term used by shady producers and filmmakers.

I tell them to steer clear of any filmmaker or producer or casting director who uses the term 'bold'; more often than not 'bold' is an excuse and a covert hint for the 'ouch couch'.

My mantra of working is simple, work only with people that match your energies with absolute clarity. I know finding matching energies is easier said than done. It is a practice actually that you perfect as you make films.

Many a times, novices in the cast and the crew want to know the budget and mode of filming. I react with a curt, "excuse me are you investing any money, I am hiring you to make the film my way". It shuts them up!

A reason could be aspiring cast and crew, even established cast and crew that can't sell a film or show on their own, is rubbed wrong many-a-times. Working on the films and shows of other producers and directors, I have seen it happen to me!

Initially, I too worked with a lot of people with toxicity. They are still living in their illusionary world without any work. On the other hand there are people ever so thankful, like few of the initial career-stage lead actors – Laila Panda, Reema Ali, Rahul Sethi and Ankit Challa – that are so very thankful to me for giving them their first break and launching them in the lead.

Practice also makes you understand the new tools of filmmaking, today when films can be made on mobile; it is not the technique, but the art of story-telling that is important. Unfortunately, 90% of filmmakers today don't know the art of storytelling – they compensate the lack of this skill with 'epithets' like Visual Story Artist, Digital Creator and other blah – point is, are they doing anything worthwhile other than there gang of five to ten people. I have IG'rs with a million followers coming to me asking for the ever-elusive break!

Today there are cameras that don't need many lights, can film very well in low-light, the in-built mic is strong enough to capture sound and you can move about a shot better in post-production then on the set. So filmmakers can even make a film with no-budget, with just a two person cast and crew; may be single-person.

All you need is to get real and tell compelling stories.

What will the make-up and the fancy costumes do, if an actor or an actress can't act. Can a great make-up or fancy clothes, bring in the emotions to connect with the audiences.

Anybody who can answer this question correctly can be a successful filmmaker for sure!

Chapter – 2B

CINEMA, MY FIRST LESSON

Now that you know what guerrilla-filmmaking is, how exactly did my guerrilla filmmaking journey start?

As already told, it was all thanks to the scum of a producer, National Award-Winning at that! Mentioned before, he wanted to steal my script, Virgin.. Mira. I challenged him on his face in his sea-facing apartment in Versova, if he had the balls, try it. I will sue such that his entire life will be f#@ked.

I mulled how to make Virgin.. Mira, as it was very important for me now, because at the back of the head, I knew I have to take the first initiative of making the film.

It was during that time that a friend who had burned about 10 million bucks on trying to make a film, only realizing that the director was just taking him for a ride with that 'film'; told me that he will make the film.

The problem was, he wanted me to shoot the film at a tourist destination and Virgin.. Mira could only be shot in India in its present script-form. He offered to produce Virgin.. Mira, if I shot a film for him at the tourist destination – I Am A Love Addict was born.

These two films were possible only because of Guerrilla filmmaking.

I knew Virgin.. Mira was just the right film to kickstart my filmmaking career, I Am A Love Addict – icing on the cake – but Guerrilla Films, I was still perplexed.

Before I recount how I did away with the huge block of guerrilla-filmmaking, let me tell you one fact of the film-industry that no one will, with a simple one word statement.

Making films is all about the network you have. Selling films is all about the network you have.

I got one of the most saleable stars from Hollywood to launch the reboot of '69 Opposites Attract'. Dominique Swain did the honors.

How did I get Dominique Swain?

All thanks to the network that I have developed in a decade and a half!

Chapter – 4

Put Away the Mental-Block Amitabh Bachchan, Raj Kapoor, Dev Anand and James Cameron

Doing away with the huge block of guerrilla-filmmaking was very, very tough!

Though I knew Virgin.. Mira was just the right film to kickstart my filmmaking career; but starting my career making guerrilla-films was what I was unsure of.

In my previous book, I had detailed the way four people had an everlasting impact on me and my film-making career – Amitabh Bachchan, Raj Kapoor, Dev Anand and James Cameron.

All of these had an indelible impression on my filmmaking style, rather beliefs and my outlook on making films in particular.

Still, like all filmmakers I was at the uncertainty cliff, whether to wait eternally for 'the star' to bestow his blessings on me and my film and hence help me get a producer onboard or to make B-grade stuff.

Around this time I read James Cameron's now famous quote on filmmaking:

Pick up a camera. Shoot something.

No matter how small, no matter how cheesy.

No matter whether your friends or sister star in it.

Put your name on it.

Now you are a Director

Everything after that is negotiating your budget and your fee

I also watched one of the interviews of legendary Raj Kapoor, in which he famously said:

Achchi filmein banti nahin hain, bann jaati hain

Translation: Good films are not made, they just get made

These two statements and the fact what Mr. Bachchan always say that as an artist I am continually struggling and striving to better my work and I will do whatever opportunities I get that showcases the artist in me, helped me firm up my mind. It moved me from that cliff of uncertainty to concrete action!

I realized I can't make B-grade stuff, and I can no longer wait for the stars in the 'cat and mouse' game. Inspired by the quote of the man who made World's first US$ 1Bn movie, Titanic and World's first US$ 2Bn movie Avatar, James Cameron, I decided to start making guerrilla films.

And Popcorn Flicks was firmly established!

My reasoning of starting my career with guerrilla films was James Cameron. Making two highest-grossing films couldn't be a fluke. I am not even using the word probably, when I say he is the filmmaker to make World's first US$ 3Bn movie, it will happen with Avatar – The Way of Water. Post-pandemic the biz has changed, if it does US$ 2Bn it is equivalent to US$ 3.6Bn in reality!

Another reason was, I saw the history of first AD's in India. They grow from energetic 20-year self to 70 years olds – waiting for the stars to make a film and with due respect to them and their choice; I definitely didn't want to end up like them.

Today, I am very happy that I took the plunge, because James Cameron was so right. Today I find it's all about negotiating the budget and the fees. I am a sought after film-consultant today, it is all because I started making guerrilla films.

Popcorn Flicks, today, is invited by various countries and film-commissions to initiate the first concrete step and forge the film-making relations between India and their country.

This picture is from the filming of 1st Indo-Kyrgyz feature film. Reason I chose it is because, I experienced the power of cinema first hand. They opened this massive 1000-seater auditorium for me to film, all because of Raj Kapoor!

The name of the character I played in the film is Honey Kapoor, the people in Russia and CIS countries connected Kapoor to Raj Kapoor and everyone went berserk!

Ladies as old as 70 and 80 that couldn't walk without a stick got up and wanted to be clicked with me, all because of Raj Kapoor!

Hats-off to this man who was the first to put India on the global map!

Slowly, when people got to know that I was delivering films, many small time indie-producers with very limited budgets, started forging alliances with me. I have got a Polish filmmaker coming all the way from Poland, to make a film in India in 2023.

Coming to guerrilla films, these were for the international film festival circuit, in essence very bollywood-ish, yet not quite bollywood.

This unique style and narrative resulted in creation of three cult films made within 9-months of each other, Virgin.. Mira, I Am A Love Addict and 69 Opposites Attract.

As it happens with all experiments, the films were treated as 'cult' in the international market, opening unimaginable avenues for me as a filmmaker.

My quest for experimentation made me the first filmmaker to release a feature film simultaneously on YouTube. YouTube was still in nascent stage in 2009, '69 Opposites Attract' was the Top YouTube performer in Entertainment for four-weeks in a row!

Like all people I too made a mistake, I let this success wane away in thin-air. I stopped using YouTube from 2009 to 2018 – the years when YouTube really grew! That's life.

These films were possible only because of Guerrilla filmmaking.

I Am A Love Addict premiered at the legendary Village East Cinemas, New York; where Abel Ferrara said that my filmmaking style is so like Woody Allen's. Virgin.. Mira premiered during the Cannes Film Festival.

Chapter – 5

CANNES FILM FESTIVAL AND THE TOP-10 FILM FESTS

No book on film, no career of a filmmaker and no filmography of an actor; can ever be complete without the mention of Cannes Film Festival.

When I made Virgin.. Mira, one thing was very clear from the onset that the film has go to the biggest film-event on planet earth – Cannes.

Today Cannes is a must-have if you want to be remembered as a film-professional after you are long gone. Hundred years or two-hundred years down the line.

How did I discover Cannes Film Festival?

I was at crossroads what to do with my filmmaking ambitions. It was during this time I started viewing films from the Top-10 film festivals of the world. I feel if you really want to make films and are serious about it, watching films from Top-10 film festivals of the world is very important.

The films at these top-10 film festivals opened me up with their in-your-face realism.

Some of the films also came as a sheer shock and attack on my morality, the upper middle-class morality to be precise. The films like Lars von Trier's The Idiots, Dogville, Anti-Christ in particular followed by Nymphomaniac, Gasper Noe's Love and the very controversial Palme d'Or winner, Blue Is The Warmest Colour – replete with explicit nudity and sex-scenes made me wonder, is it a film or just an excuse to make porn?

An actress and a filmmaker based in London eased me up with the quote, "One Man's Pornography is Another Man's High Art."

Cannes was right at the top of these Top-10 film festivals and leads the Top-10 by quite a margin! My first Cannes Film Festival with Virgin.. Mira and another of my 'now cult' film, 69 Opposites Attract was an eye-opener.

It made me clear without any doubt that films is a product and like all products they have buyers, it is all about finding the right buyer for your product. Cannes Film Festival together with the top-10 film festivals for sure, are the best film-school to go to.

These films teach you a lot. The distinct styles, myriad narratives and a total uninhibited, unconventional approach will change your entire perspective of cinema. It really broadens your horizon as a filmmaker.

Coming back to Cannes Film Festival that even a kid today knows about, thanks to the crazy media-frenzy that go to insane heights to write who wore what with photo-bombing splashes across the glitzy pages both in print and online. But, do any of these Indian celebrities, read actresses, really make a splash or is it all the great Indian media hogwash?

Frankly, the big-3 at the Cannes Film Festival – Variety, The Hollywood Reporter and Screen Weekly, publish only one Indian – Aishwarya Rai. Over the years since 2003, Ash seems to have reversed the roles where she doesn't represent *Bollywood* – but *Bollywood in Cannes* means Aishwarya Rai. That is her clout, firmly etched, even after two decades.

Rest of the actresses can take heart from the fact that Indian media is kind and hail them as the Red-Carpet scorchers, only if they really were!

In 2023, it will be my 14th Cannes and in these 14 years, never once have I been able to complete the Cannes Film Festival and Film Market in entirety – that is the scale and size of Cannes, even 11-days are not enough to cover it in entirety.

Having said that my first Cannes, taught me a lot about film-sales; first lesson as I already mentioned was, film is a product and each product is saleable. All you need to do is identify buyers. It is very tricky, but not impossible.

Do your homework before you go to Cannes though, because if you want to make an impression, be ready to fork out anywhere around five to six lacs, minimum.

The experience I got from my first Cannes Film Festival also changed my film-making approach radically. I was now doing pre-sales or initiating sales and then designing the film, to limit losses, if any.

Interestingly, Cannes Film Festival was also instrumental in bringing out the real actor in me. I was already an actor with Virgin.. Mira; my first act ever in front of camera that interestingly was the lead role!

But it was at Cannes really that I became a full-fledged actor.

I met an Italian filmmaker Margarita, now a dear friend. Hailed as the new-age auteur, she wanted me to play lead in her movie.

I told her I am a default actor. I had already played the lead role of Raghav Krishna in Virgin.. Mira.

Interestingly, it was the lead actress, Reema Ali that insisted I play the role as she was comfortable acting only opposite me.

Coming back to Margarita, she told me that anybody can act, when directing self, being directed by a director is a challenge.

I didn't really want to act, but since she was setting her film in Cannes and I was saving a lot of money because the entire edition of Cannes was sponsored by her. I took up the offer.

This film and the role really taught me the finer nuances of an international production. But this role was really going to be a real test of my nerves as I was soon going to know.

Chapter – 6

My First Nude Scene

The real challenge in Margarita's film was not acting, but performing my first nude scene.

Before I write further, I have an interesting anecdote to share. Virgin.. Mira had a nude scene. It was at the point where the man meets the girl auctioning her virginity for the first time. Reema and I had a lot of discussions on the script; nude-scenes in particular, when we staged the scene during rehearsals. After a lot of discussions and watching few Palme d'Or winners, we decided to tone it down to light intimacy.

This was a grossly wrong decision; I was soon going to know, because when the buyers at Marche du Film, Cannes Film Festival saw the film they were aghast. They were like, you need to create an impact with your film, the audience will invest more if they related with the characters. You are talking about virginity, about them getting intimate and there is no nudity or even intimacy. The light intimacy you have onscreen is diluting the impact of the film.

Their feedback at that point didn't make me realize the importance of intimacy and onscreen nudity in visual arts; I simply couldn't understand their views, but after doing Margarita's film I could relate to the buyers' views.

Coming back to Margarita's film; the general view in the industry is that nude scenes are tough for women. The fact is; it's the other way around. Women are much more comfortable and natural doing nudity onscreen compared to men!

I have an analytical mind that is what my friends in the film frat say!

So I tried to figure out why women are more natural doing nude scenes and I found that probably men are much more conscious about body-shaming and the insecurity showing their unshapely figures onscreen.

Though Margarita narrated the script to me and mentioned the character I am playing will be nude, I thought it to be implied nudity; whereas, she wanted to show real nudity in the three sex scenes that she planned in the movie.

Since, I was in Europe only for 25-days, she knew, she will have to help me overcome my inhibitions real quick.

She started by talking. She told me Indians were the most open in the matters of sexuality. Kamasutra is the most famous text that is regarded as sacred the worldover. Moreover, just like we act, we are acting our part by doing intimate scenes!

Almost all the superstars have done it worldwide. Many Indian actors have done nudity as well, starting with one of the most illustrious superstars, again a Kapoor, Shashi Kapoor.

Her talk eased me up a lot!

The way she handled it all, helped me a lot when I directed intimacy onscreen.

In fact, it is only because of Margarita that I became the first intimacy director in Asia. Well, if not the first, one of the first.

I casually mentioned it to Margarita, and she was like 'what the hell is intimacy director. There is no such credit in films.'

After the #MeToo movement, the term 'Intimacy Director' not only got credence, but today most of the studio films employ intimacy directors to direct intimacy, nudity and sex-scenes onscreen.

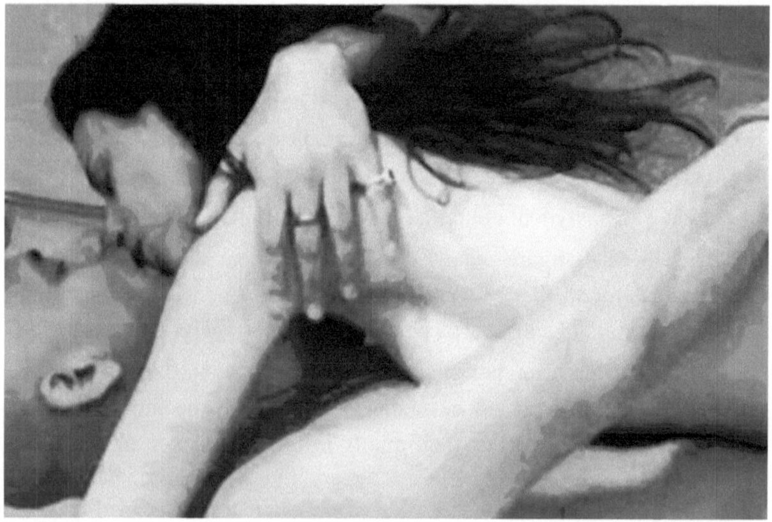

Frankly, I feel this is just a fad that will die out. I mean aren't we questioning the capabilities of a director when we employ Intimacy Director?

Do we mean to say Bernardo Bertolucci did a bad job in Last Tango in Paris or The Dreamers?

Or Paul Verhoeven was inept to direct Basic Instinct that immediately shot Sharon Stone, after years of her struggle, to superstardom.

Many actresses I have met have said that if something untoward is supposed to happen, it will happen even if the film has an Intimacy Director.

What about many independent films that can't afford an Intimacy Director and have sex and nudity as the core subject?

Will the intimacy cease to exist from films and media?

And what about the core issue, #MeToo movement, how many of those accused in Indian Film Industry by actresses were investigated upon or faced any action. How come, a director went on to be a contestant, on the Indian version of Big Brother franchise?

Frankly, almost all top actors in Hollywood and superstars have done nude scenes, I personally feel, providing safer work environment is the best solution, then to digress, the core issue by hiring Intimacy Directors.

Coming back to Margarita's movie, I had a fleeting glimpse of the nude scene from the movie in my acting reel. This acting reel somehow made its way into the phones of my, well, the infamous nosy Indian aunties (what the f@#k were they searching for?)

They gossiped about the nude scene together with much of salt 'n' pepper, with my mother.

Normally, I don't do this, but since two of the many aunties seemed to have got the shots of testosterone; I had to calm them down with the fact that their respective daughter-in-laws have f@#%ked half of the guys in the city after getting sloshed.

That shut them up. Not only them but all the nosy aunties for good.

Why is this crab mentality and hypocrisy so firmly ingrained in the people of the Indian sub-continent?

Today I am a sought after panelist on cinema, media and culture on the national news-broadcasters.

देश का बेस्ट डिबेट शो 'राष्ट्रवाद'
:27 3,160 views
SAHARA
SAHARA

Chapter – 7

FILM MARKETS

Film markets are simply the place where one can buy or sell films.

The beauty of cinema is that the journey of each film-professional is unique.

Similarly, each film is unique and has got a sales-potential.

I knew given the subject-matter Virgin.. Mira will work internationally. Since the sales-agents were asking hefty-fees upfront I had to take the film to film markets.

Virgin.. Mira together with 69 Opposites Attract helped me discover film-markets.

The major film festivals have a very established film market that goes on together with the festival and is the backbone of any film festival.

Case in point:

Cannes Film Festival is *the Cannes* because of a very developed and evolved film market. The activity at Marche du Film of Cannes Film Festival supersedes the activity of the entire 11-day film festival.

My first impression at the first market at the Cannes Film Festival that I attended was that of an unwanted Indian film-maker!

I learned this in 3-days flat. No one was interested to deal with me and when they got to know that I am from India, they were like we don't want Indian films. This was in 2009.

So after the third day, I changed my strategy. I had a quick pitch of 30-seconds ready.

"Hi, I am an Indian filmmaker with an indie film, "69 Opposites Attract". Will it interest you?"

Point was, this pitch changed the outlook of people they started to be polite and at least acknowledged my presence!

Since no one bought the film, I decided to party, which is another struggle.

I went to get an invite for the party of a Latin American country. The receptionist told me, she has finished all the invites. Just then an old gentleman started talking to me.

Since I have always had a very open and receptive outlook towards life, I started chatting with him.

When I told him about the film's title, '69 Opposites Attract'; he was like 'what is the film about?'

Me – *It is about the perennial global question, 'can a boy and a girl really just be good friends?'*

He – *And what did you find?*

Me (with a smile) – *For that you will have to see the film*

He smiled and the smile flashed all over his wrinkled yet distinctly glowing face.

I knew instantly, I have made my first success at the very first Cannes Film Festival!

Did business with him for two of my films, 'Virgin.. Mira' and '69 Opposites Attract'.

I got to know he was the leading distributor in the ABC of Latin American countries, Argentina, Brazil, Chile!

He introduced me to his network and helped me with the distribution of *Virgin Mira* and *69 Opposites Attract.*

Slowly and gradually, I developed a network.

From film-maker I metamorphosed into a complete film-professional.

By 2015, I was being invited to the most happening parties at the Cannes Film Festival only because of the business I generated.

I was helping many Independent producers and actors with positioning themselves at the Cannes Film Festival with the right fit, helping them develop a quality network.

I also realized the basic fault of 90% producers!

Most of the producers spend the entire budget on making films; they didn't have even a few thousand dollars to market films.

Today more than making a film, it is the marketing of a film that requires real money.

Another thing that I learned at Cannes Film Festival was, each and every film is saleable, all you need is, to know the people. The buyers that would buy your film, this is the real job. As I mentioned earlier, in 14 years I haven't been able to cover Cannes Film festival in full, it's so huge.

Probably, this is the reason there are so many consultants offering their services at the Cannes Film Festival.

Chapter – 8

THE BUSINESS OF CINEMA

This section will be real short as the gist of 'The Business of Cinema' is already covered in the Chapter 7.

Many independent producers and even studio-execs spend a lifetime understanding business of cinema. It is pretty simple to understand. The thumb-rule is, if a producer makes ten films, seven will lose money, three will make money – but the money these three films will make will be enough to make ten more films.

This cycle continues!

Analyze any studio worldwide be it Hollywood, Hindi Film Industry or any industry. This model is the ground reality.

Another reality is the fact that a film might not work in one market, but it can always work in another market.

Case in point:

Sanjay Leela Bhansali's Guzaarish starring Hrithik Roshan and Aishwarya Rai, while it was a flop in India, in South Korea the film had 1-million admissions!

You can make money even from your flop films, if you know how to distribute your films and content in the best optimal manner.

Next time if your film flops, don't be depressed; find the markets that will work for your film, play your film in as many film festivals as you can!

No one knows the opportunities that might open with increased visibility of the film.

Today, I am rebooting Virgin.. Mira, it is already being done as a show internationally.

In India too, few production-houses are exploring ways to make it.

Films are digital, today. The ease of making films is very much there, but the block of marketing films is widening. No wonder today then, more and more filmmakers are realizing that more than 'making the film', it is about 'marketing the film'.

Most people think that marketing the film right is all about reaching the target-audiences.

Marketing in todays' context is not just reaching your target-audiences, but adding on to your target-audiences by reaching the unexplored markets. The picture below is from a city-square in Italy, the frenzy of fans I saw there will put the biggest superstars to shame.

How many events have you planned for your under-production film?

Very recently a friend made a US$ One Million film, co-produced by a mid-level actress. I told him at the very onset when he started the film, keep the budget for marketing; but as with all filmmakers he spent all the money on making. Result film is stuck since two years for release.

In my MasterClasses on cinema worldwide, I always lay stress on marketing films, few that understand make their second film. Those that don't, well they are still struggling to release their first film.

Chapter 9
MY PROUD MOMENT

While there have been chapters at the start of the book on both the Cannes Film Festival and Amitabh bachchan. I am bringing them again here, because after detailing the high of Raj Kapoor in Kyrgyzstan; it is very important to tell you the high of Amitabh Bachchan at Cannes.

But before that, in my 14 years, I have decoded the myth of Cannes Film Festival, why is it so popular?

Why of all the top-10 film fests, Cannes is the name that comes right as the first name by default?

The answer is – Cannes has magic. The magic of turning nobodies into stars, launching careers!

Will you walk up to a girl and say I want to cast you in my film. I did just that in Cannes, because I saw the girl in the picture at a café. She had a very composed face and the look I wanted for a particular film. I just went up to her, the next day we did a small audition that turned into a film and bingo, she did six-films with me over the next five years.

She was picked up by a German director, after he saw her work in one of the films we did together. I still have vivid memories of the thanks she gave me. She hired a yacht and threw a party to thank me!

Reason we stopped, rather she stopped working was, her husband didn't want her to continue with acting. She and I are still very good friends, she divorced during the pandemic and hopefully she will return to films soon.

This brings me back to Virgin.. Mira and Reema Ali; I still vividly remember her excitement when I told her Virgin.. Mira will be going to Cannes. I still remember her showing me her dress for the Red-Carpet and chuckling Aishwarya Rai has got stiff competition this year!

She couldn't go to Cannes Film Festival, though she so much wanted to go to Cannes. This reminds me of what Woody Allen told me – only destiny gets you to Cannes!

Seems she planned to get married. Eventually because of my super-busy scheds we lost touch. I hope and pray that she is leading a happily married life now.

If you want to succeed in the film industry, the only point is to stay focused till you find success. Of course, the meaning and perspective of success differs.

When I asked Dev Anand, how does it feel after making cult films like Hare Rama Hare Krishna, Des Pardes and many more to making films like Chargesheet, Censor, Sau Crore – without a single success for almost three-decades (In 2011, just after the release of Chargesheet) he smiled and said, "Amit even if one person sees my film, I will continue making films."

This one statement is a MasterClass in Cinema!

I have no clue, how many fans I have made worldwide, but one thing I know for sure is, wherever I go I connect, wherever I speak, I connect. People rush to me to get pictures clicked, as you can see in the picture below, after my masterclass on cinema in Kyrgyzstan.

Coming back to Cannes and Bachchan; the year was 2013.

The film was The Great Gatsby.

The film was brilliantly directed by Baz Luhrmann and acted by Leonardo DiCaprio and Tobey Maguire; Mr. Bachchan had a small cameo in the film. Yet at Cannes, he was treated and given the protocol of the lead cast in the film.

That is the power a superstar ought to wield.

The real surprise, though, waited for all at the Grand Lumiere as the film was the Opening Film of the 2013-edition. Indians particularly were taken by surprise!

Bachchan spoke in chaste Hindi; there was a French interpreter and English interpreter with Leo, Tobey, Margot Robbie listening to Bachchan in rapt attention and after the speech the whole of the Grand Lumiere rose up, to give Bachchan a standing ovation!

That was the moment I really felt proud as an Indian!

That was the moment I really felt proud to be a part of the Indian film fraternity.

Again, it was the power of the mindset and the mental health that in spite of doing a small cameo, Bachchan made the role big enough to get the top-billing only with his persona!

The same view was endorsed by Baz in the press-conference to a query from a journalist, as he asked Baz, why he chose an Indian actor in the role of a Jew; over so many other actors including some legendary Jewish actors.

Chapter 10
THE GIST

The gist of all the mastercalsses and workshops in cinema, entertainment and media industry that I have attended in my 15-year career is that it's all about funds.

I had the good fortune of interacting with Academy-Award winning actor Sir Ben Kingsley, while everyone was falling over each other to get a picture clicked with him. I sat on the chair right in front of him smiling.

After five minutes he asked me, are you an actor. I replied that I am primarily a filmmaker, but now I do practically everything related to cinema including cinmeatogarphy and editing.

He smiled and asked me what gets me to Cannes Film Festival.

I told him funds, he smiled and said that's the reason he was there too. We both had a hearty laugh.

He then told me about his dream project, 'Taj Mahal' and how he is raising US$ 50Mn for the film. He was very sure he wanted only Aishwarya Rai to play Mumtaz Mahal.

Well, I wish him all the luck for Taj Mahal.

Chapter 11

THE FIRST DRAFT–SCREENPLAY (2001)

Before I leave you with the screenplay (almost the shooting script of Virgin.. Mira) that I wrote while I was still in college; I want to share something I am always proud of and forever thankful to – my audiences that are spread all over the world in all the continents that planet earth has.

Yes, I pride myself over this fact!

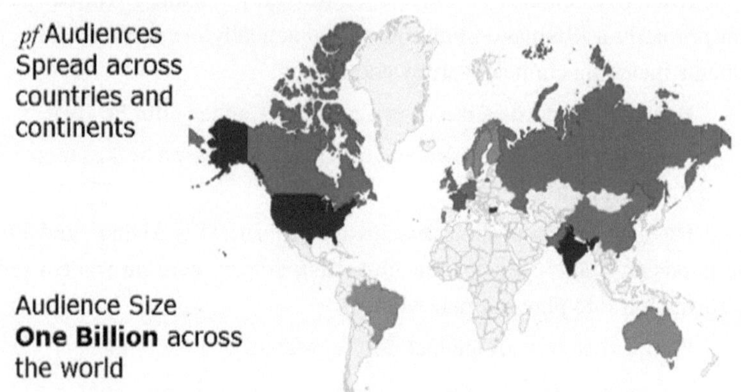

And finally, here it is..

Giving you a complete recap of
the making of Virgin.. Mira
right from the ideation, to pitching to production, to release, to marketing of the film
– I am leaving all the readers with the first draft of the screenplay of the film,
it is in fact, more than just the screenplay
it is the shooting script in essence
of course the screenplay from 2006 to 2022 has seen a drastic change,
till you see the 2022 version, here is the 2006 draft of the screenplay – the first draft

Virgin… Mira
By Amit R Agarwal

(The dialogues are in Hindi written in English for ex: क्या is written as Kya)

Scene – 1

We open with the ringing of a mobile

A hand picks up the mobile

We show the side profile of the mobile glued on to an ear

Subhashini – voice

Mein social activist Subhashini bol rahee hoon… Mein aapse Mira Ali ke baare mein kuch baat karna chahti hoon…

Dissolve to

Scene – 2

Newspaper / news channel office. We establish the working atmosphere in the office.

Dissolve to

From the vapors coming off two cups of steaming coffees we pull out to reveal two cups of coffees kept in front of Nirbhay and DINESH; they sit facing each other, DINESH speaks as he gets up to go to the window.

DINESH

Mashhoor businessman Raghav Krishna ka kal raat ko murder ho gaya hai…

NIRBHAY

Jaanta hoon…

DINESH

Aur abhi abhi mili ek khabar ke mutaabik iss murder ke liye… Mira Ali ko pakda gaya hai…

NIRBHAY *a bit shocked*

Mira Ali… aapka matlab…

DINESH

Bilkul sahee samjhay tum… Mira Ali… jo story tum uss waqt nahin kar paaye thay vo ab kar sakte ho… uss time bhi Mira kee story hot thee… aur ab iss murder ke baad to Mira kee story… smiles… dekho agar tum iss story ko break kar paao… as we charge on Nirbhay, the DINESH continues… after all badee interesting story hai… Mira Ali urf Virgin Mira kee…

Fade to black

The credit titles **Virgin Mira** appears

Credits roll on the film

Scene – 3

Caption reads: A year back
We pull out from the face of a very serious looking Nirbhay.
In another cut we show an equally serious DINESH

DINESH

Tumhaara matlab hai… ki ye jo ladki hai… Mira… ye apnee virginity bechnaa chahti hai…

NIRBHAY

Yeah…

DINESH

Are you sure…

NIRBHAY

Net per hai sir… rukiye mein aapko bhi dikhaata hoon…

Nirbhay comes to DINESH' computer… and keys in a few keys

NIRBHAY

Ye dekhiye sir…

DINESH looks at the comp
DINESH *letting out a sigh*

GOD! Hamara desh kahan jaa raha hai… ladkiyaan apnee virginity bech raheen hain…

NIRBHAY

Bech nahin… auction kar raheen hain… to the highest bidder…

DINESH

Khoobsurat hai…

NIRBHAY

Bid lagaaoon kya…

DINESH hits him lightly, both laugh lightly.

DINESH

Get me the story…

Dissolve to

Scene – 4 {flashback}

College. Mira is walking by. Nirbhay is accosting her.

NIRBHAY

Mira… you have to listen to me… tum mere sawaalon se bachkar nahin jaa saktee ho… tumhein jawab dena hee hoga ki aakhir tum kyun… apnee virginity auction karna chahti ho?

Mira turns towards Nirbhay and after a freezing stare says…

MIRA

I am not a public property… I am not answerable to you…

NIRBHAY

You are wrong… apnee virginity bechnay ka public notice nikaalkar tum public property hee bann gayee ho…

Mira stares at him. Nirbhay looks at her... Mira opens her bag and takes out a dagger... she points it at Nirbhay. Nirbhay is a bit scared.

NIRBHAY

Ye… ye tum kya kar rahee ho…

Mira walks upto him. Intercuts. Drama builds up. She looks at him. He looks at her. She lifts the dagger.

NIRBHAY thinking that she is out to stab him

Dekho kanoon ko…

He can't even complete the sentence... With a swish... Mira stabs herself. Shock on Nirbhay's face.

Mira's eyes close.

Fade to black

Nirbhay's overlap – **oh no…** *overlapped with ambulance's siren.*

Scene – 5 {flashback}

Nirbhay is sitting with his head down in DINESH' cabin. DINESH tells him, as he gives him coffee.

DINESH

Nirbhay… tum jaise star reporter se mujhe aisee immaturity kee ummeed nahin thee…

DINESH sighs

NIRBHAY

Sir maine expect hee nahin kiya thaa ki Mira apnay aapko stab kar legi…

DINESH

News mein… be ready to expect the unexpected... fact is stranger than fiction…

Nirbhay looks up at the DINESH

NIRBHAY

Sir… aagay se mein careful rahoonga…

DINESH

Tension mat lo… tumhaare achche record ke chalte mein tum per koyee action nahin le raha hoon… balki jack lagvakar police case ko bhi rafa dafa karva diya hai… aage se reporting karte time hamesha dhyaan rakhna… complex cases mein kaam shuru karnay se pahle… always break the ice…

Fade to black

Audio overlap on fade to black, ***"always break the ice"***

Scene – 6

In a posh workable flat nirbhay is walking up & down the room sipping coke from the can.

NIRBHAY

Picchli baar to galti ho gayee thee… iss baar… I have to get it right… how do I break the ice?

Dissolve to

Nitbhay keeps the can with a sound on his computer table. He is working on the computer. He mumbles – **"breaking the ice…"** *he keys in... He mumbles –* **tip 1… tip 2… tip 3…**

NIRBHAY

Hmmm… this seems to be doable…

He sits back against the back of his chair & takes a sip, he closes his eyes...

Flashcuts: *Mira stabbing herself.*

Nirbhay opens his eyes

NIRBHAY sighs

MIRA… I hope it works… picks up a dart kept on the table alongside and aims it at the dart board… Mira…

Dissolve to

Scene – 7

We show the exterior of a prison.

Dissolve to

Nirbhay is sitting with Mira... Mira is looking down on the table... Nirbhay is staring at her... build up of the cuts...

NIRBHAY

Vaise toh mujhe tumse milnay ka koyee shauq nahin thaa… per Subhashini jee ke kehnay per mere boss ne mujhe tumse milnay ke liye kaha hai…

Look of Mira

Pregnant silence follows

To tumhaare baare mein mera pehla impression sahee thaa… *mira continues looking down...* paise ke liye tum kisi hadh tak bhi jaa sakti ho… apnee virginity ka sauda tak kar saktee ho… aur ab… ab to… murder bhi kar saktee ho…

We show in 2-3 cuts on the dialogue that mira is getting angry but she continues looking down on the table…

Nirbhay gives a good look to her. He gets up and walks up to her chair.

Mira continues to look down.

He goes behind her chair and grabs hold of her as he says…

NIRBHAY

How much will you charge for a NIGHT with me?

He feels Mira rather wildly.

Mira is getting irritated & finally she frees herself

MIRA *shouts at the top of her voice*

Maine koyee khoon nahin kiya hai… nahin kiya hai… mein to bas shaanti se jeena chahti hoon… mere baare mein koyee kuch nahin jaanta hai…

NIRBHAY *as he struggles to get up*

Vohee to mein jaannay aaya hoon… tumhaari kahaani…

Dissolve to

Scene – 8

We show the exterior of a building.

Dissolve to

Nirbhay & Mira are drinking coffee...

NIRBHAY

Sorry… maine tumhaare baare mein bhala bura kaha… lekin pichchli baar kee tarah mein koyee galti nahin karna chahta thaa… I just wanted to break the ice…

Now Mira looks in Nirbhay's eyes...

Kal maine net per ek article pada thaa… ussmein likha thaa ki kisi ko humiliate karna bhi ice ko break kar sakta hai… uskee chuppi ko todh sakta hai… and it worked…

Mira looks up

Mein chahta hoon ki mein tumhaari sachchi kahaani logon tak pahunchaaoon…

Look of Mira

Aur iskay liye tumhein apnee kahaani mujhe bataani padegi… sabkuch… ekdum sach sach…

Mira looks at nirbhay as if gauging him. Nirbhay holds her hand and gives her a reassuring look.

NIRBHAY

Mein jaanta hoon iss duniya ne samay samay per tumhaare vishwaas ko toda hai… per tum mujhper bharosa kar saktee ho… I want to help you…

Mira looks at him, her reserve softens up. She has a slight smile on her face.

NIRBHAY

Ek compliment doon… you have a beautiful smile…

Mira's smile brighten up…

NIRBHAY

Bas… smile karne mein agar itnee kanjoosi nahin karogi… to tumhaari beautiful smile the most beautiful smile bann jaayegi…

Mira smiles

NIRBHAY

Good… haan to maine poocha…

Just then there is an audio overlap – milnay ka waqt khatm ho chukka hai…

Nirbhay looks at Mira

NIRBHAY

Mein tumse milnay kal aaoonga… tum mujhse milogi naa…

Mira looks at Nirbhay and nods her head

NIRBHAY

Mein tumhaari aawaaz sunna chahta hoon…

MIRA

Haan… miloongi…

Cut to

Scene – 9

Mira is sitting on the chair with her hands resting on the table. Nirbhay comes in munching on a burger.

NIRBHAY

Sorry… mein thoda late ho gaya… kya karoon… busy schedules… pulls the chair and sits… he keeps a Dictaphone on the table & says… to bataao apnee story…

He takes a bite from the burger… Mira looks at the burger… Nirbhay realises it… he eyes the burger and looks at Mira…

NIRBHAY

Wanna have a bite…

Mira literally grabs the burger and eats it hungrily.

Nirbhay looks at her wonders to himself

NIRBHAY VO thinks to himself

Kitni simple see ladki hai… aakhir kya hai iski complex story…

Cut: Mira eating burger

Dissolve to

Mira starts telling her story

Dissolve to

Scene – 10

Night. The camera pans and tilts from the skyline & establishes the city – Delhi.
In a wide shot we see a lot of buildings.
The voiceover starts as the screen fades up.

MIRA: VO

Dilli shaher mein mein… unn kayee ladkiyon mein se ek hoon jo ki chhote shahar se aatin hain… zindagi mein apna mukaam paane ke liye… mera naam Mira hai… Mein ek musalmaan hoon…

Continues her story

Scene – 11

Exterior shot of the prison meeting room

Dissolve to

Mira is telling her story

MIRA

Mere paida honay se pahle hee abbu ammi ko lekar bahrain chalay gaye thay… vahan per kaam achcha chal raha thaa… per kismet ka pher… ek dinn sabkuch khatm ho gaya aur abbu ko vaapas India aana pada… roti roti ko mohtaaz hona pada…

Dissolve to

Scene – 12

Night. Abbu is working at bakery

MIRA: VO

India aaker Abbu ne ek bakery kholi… jo ki koyee khaas chalti nahin thee…

Cut to

Scene – 13

Night. Mira is doing Namaaz.

MIRA: VO

Abbu aur ammi ke alaava, mera ek bada bhai thaa… ASLAM… Aslam ko hamaare ilaake ke maulvi ne behka diya thaa… Aslam aatankwaadi bann gaya thaa… uska kuch ata pata nahin thaa… ghar ka kharch ammi aur abbu milkar chalaate thay…

Abbu Aslam ko to kho chukay thay… issliye Abbu chahte thay ki mein padh-likhkar kuch bann jaaoon…

ABBU

Arey Fareeda ye chhape to bahut achche banaaye hain…

FAREEDA

Ye chhape maine nahin… Mira ne banaaye hain…

Abbu looks at Mira, she has finished her namaaz…
Abbu then looks at Fareeda

ABBU says in a slightly angry tone

Fareeda… pet kaat-kaat kar… mein ek-ek rupya jama kar raha hoon… *pauses*... pyaaz ke saath roti khaata hoon… kyunki mein chahta hoon ki Mira padh-likh kar kuch banay… jo kaalikh Aslam ne mere mooh per poti hai… usay saaf karay… aur tum… *pauses*... Mira se idhar udhar ka koyee bhi kaam mat karvaaya karo…

MIRA

Abbu… maine khud ye chhape taiyaar kiye hain… ammi ne mujhse koyee kaam nahin karvaaya hai… aur aap tension mat lo… mein jaanti hoon ki mere liye iss waqt sabse zaroori cheez padaayee hee hai…

Charge on Abbu
Charge on Mira
Charge on Ammi

Scene – 14

We pull out from the face of Ammi
We show Ashraf is looking at the designs intently

ASHRAF

Ye designs to bahut achche hain… *look of Ammi…* Fareeda… tumhaara kaam maine dekha hai… ye kaam tumhaara toh nahin hai…

AMMI

Ye chhape Mira ne taiyaar kiye hain…

Ashraf looks at Mira
Then he looks at Ammi

ASHRAF

Mein chahta hoon ki aagay ke designs bhi Mira hee taiyaar karay…

Ammi looks at Ashraf

AMMI

Ye ho nahin paayega… kyunki Mira ke abbu chahte hain… ki Mira doctor ya engineer banay…

ASHRAF

Doctor ya engineer… kaafi rupya lagta hai, doctor ya engineer bannay ke liye… ye designs achche hain… agar Mira mujhe designs banakar degi to mein tumhein achcha paisa doonga…

AMMI

Ye ho nahin paayega…

Charge on Ammi's firm face

Charge on Mira

Dissolve to

Scene – 15

We pull out from the face of Mira
Look of Nirbhay

NIRBHAY

Hmmm… tumhaare Abbu chahte thay ki tum padho… vo apna pait kaat-kaat kar tumhaari padhaayee ke liye rupya ikaththa kar rahay thay… zaahir hai vo tumse bahut pyar karte hongay… to phir aakhir aisee kya baat huyee… jo ki tumnay apnee virginity ko auction karnay ka thaan liya… AUR tumhaare Abbu ne kaise react kiya?

Mira's eyes moisten up as she speaks

MIRA

Abbu to tab react karte agar vo zinda hotay…

Stunned silence

NIRBHAY

Kya hua thaa tumhaare Abbu ko?

Dissolve to

Scene – 16

Night. The bakery is done up in a festive manner. We show Fareeda walking in the bakery, as she walks past she crosses a couple of people eating on a charpoy.

MIRA: VO

Mere birthday kee raat kee baat hai… Ammi Abbu ko bulaane bakery gayeen theen…

FAREEDA

Aaj ke dinn to kaam chhod do…

ABBU

Ye kaam… jo mein kar raha hoon naa… bahut hee zaroori hai… dekho Mira ke liye maine cake banaaya hai…

We show the cake
The visual is overlapped by the police-siren
Abbu's look towards the police jeep
We show the jeeps parked
The people eating on the charpoy immediately draw out gun
Shots of gun are heard **{Visual – Prison meeting room: A troubled Mira closes her ears}**
As we return to bakery we see the dead bodies, Fareeda lies dead, Abbu lies injured, we charge on him, he closes his eyes.

Fade to black

Scene – 17

Abbu is being rushed through the corridor on a stretcher.
His eyes are open. He is intently looking at Mira.

MIRA: VO

Abbu kee aankhein ek tak mujhi ko dekh raheen theen… maano ki keh raheen hon… beti… mere khwaab ko haqeeqat zaroor banana…

Abbu closes his eyes

Dissolve to

Scene – 18

Mira is sobbing lightly
Just then there is an audio overlap – **milnay ka waqt khatm ho chukka hai**…
Nirbhay sighs
He lightly holds Mira's hands and consoles her

NIRBHAY

Mein tumsay kal milnay aaoonga… he is about to leave… can I get you something…

MIRA *looks in anticipation at Nirbhay*

Burger…

NIRBHAY

Done… *smiles…*

Mira smiles back...

Cut to

Scene – 19

Nirbhay is making notes on the computer, just then Nisha calls up.

INTERCUT

Scene – 20

NISHA *visibly excited*

Hi…

NIRBHAY

Hi…

NISHA *visibly excited*

Aaj raat ek badee happening party hai… chalna hai?

NIRBHAY

Nahin babes… busy… kaam… may be some other night…

NISHA

DINESH ne aakhir tumhein aisa kya kaam de diya hai?

NIRBHAY

Kaisi journalist ho tum… itnee bhi khabar nahin hai… I am doing RATHER cracking the story of Mira Ali…

NISHA

Ahnnn… smiles… Ciao…

Nirbhay keeps the phone down

Dissolve to

Scene – 21

A top /_ shot of Nirbhay & Mira

MIRA

Aaj tumhaara camera kahan hai?

NIRBHAY

Gone for repairs…

Look of Nirbhay

MIRA

Poocho… tumhein kya poochna hai?

NIRBHAY

Tumhaare abbu kee maut ke baad kya hua?

Look of Mira

MIRA

Abbu aur ammi kee maut ke baad mein bilkul akeli ho gayee… tanha…

NIRBHAY

Kyun… tumhaare rishtedaar vagairah…

MIRA laughs lightly in a sarcastic manner…

Rishtedaar… inn rishton vagairah ko to bas ek naam de diya gaya hai… museebat ke waqt koyee kaam mein nahin aata hai…

NIRBHAY

Matlab? Tumhaare rishtedaaron ne tumhaari koyee madad nahin kee…

Mira nods in negative as her eyes moisten up

MIRA

Nahin… ulta… mere abbu aur meri ammi kee maut ka mujhe jo compensation mila… ussper bhi unhonay haath saaf kar diya…

Look of Nirbhay

Scene – 30 BAKERY NIGHT

Night. Mira looks at the bakery teary eyed

MIRA: VO

Bakery ko bhi bakery maalik ne mujhse khaali karva liya… ab mere paas kuch bhi nahin bacha thaa…

NIRBHAY

Hmmm… toh… apna kharcha chalaane ke liye hee tumnay apnee virginity…

Mira looks in infinity as her eyes moisten up

MIRA

Nahin… abhi nahin… Abbu aur Ammi ke jaane ke teen maheenay baad… college se mera naam kaat diya gaya… mere paas fees dene ke liye paise nahin thay… Aisay mein… mere hee college ka ek ladka Rahul mere paas aaya…

NIRBHAY

Boyfriend!?

Mira laughs a light sarcastic laugh

MIRA

Boyfriend…

She looks in infinity

A jerk… *sighs*…

Scene – 22

RAHUL

Hey Mira mujhe tumhaare baare mein pata chala… tumhaare saath jo ho raha hai… sahee nahin ho raha hai… ye lo ye paise rakho… aur fees bhar do…

Mira looks at Rahul

RAHUL

Bright student ho… tumhein poora dil lagakar achche se padaayee karnee chahiye tumhaara future bahut bright hai…

MIRA

Thanks Rahul…

RAHUL

Hey… friends ek doosre ko thanks nahin kehtay hai…

Rahul smiles

Mira smiles

Scene – 23

Rahul & Mira walking through the corridor in various dissolves

MIRA: VO

Rahul kee vajah se mera lifestyle thoda behtar ho gaya… maine ek PG bhi le liya… dheeray dheeray Rahul aur mein ek doosre ke kareeb aate gaye… I got a feeling… that everything will be alright now… ek raat Rahul aur mein ek party se laut rahay thay…

Scene – 24

Night. We show Rahul with Mira in the car
Rahul is looking at Mira

RAHUL

Hey Mira… raaste mein ek hotel hai… nothing great… but manageable… wanna check it out…

MIRA

No way…

Rahul looks at Mira, then he smiles and goes dreamy eyed

Dissolve to

Lead in to SONG 1

SONG 1

Scene – 24 A

Night. We show Rahul with Mira in the car

Achaanak Rahul ne car rok dee…

MIRA

Kya hua Rahul… car kyun rok dee…

RAHUL looking at Mira's tits

Mira you have got nice danglers…

MIRA adjusting her danglers

Thanks…

RAHUL

I want to have a closer look…

Mira gives a look to Rahul
Rahul unbuttons her top
Mira looks at Rahul aghast

MIRA

Rahul…

RAHUL

Shhh…

He plants his lips on Mira's lips

MIRA

Rahul stop…

RAHUL

Sooner or later… we have to do this… c'mon…

Mira pushes Rahul off

MIRA

Rahul NO…

Mira gets off the car

Rahul sighs and comes out too

RAHUL

Hey kya hua? You are my friend… it's OK…

MIRA

Rahul I am not ready for this…

RAHUL

Oh… bhaav khaa rahee ho… paise aur chahiye?

Mira is extremely hurt, she looks at Rahul

RAHUL

Naa shakl hai… naa surat hai… phir bhi itnay bhaav… mere paise kab vaapas karogi…

MIRA looks away from Rahul

Kar doongi…

RAHUL

Hmmm… ciao…

Mira looks at Rahul
Rahul gets in the car and speeds off…
Mira stands there in the night absolutely scared, she looks here and there

MIRA: VO

Uss raat pehli baar mujhe ehsaas hua… ki ek ladki ke liye ye zindagi kitni mushkil hoti hai…

Scene – 25

We show Mira entering the jewelry store

MIRA: VO

Rahul ke rupaye vaapas karne ka mujhe ek hee raasta samajh mein aaya… Ashraf ko designs bana kar doon…

We show Ashraf is looking at the designs intently

ASHRAF

Good… pulls out a wad of notes… ye lo…

MIRA

Thanks…

Mira walks out. Ashraf looks at her leaving the store

MIRA: VO

Designs ke unn rupayon se maine ek chhota saa flat rent kar liya… aur mein regularly Ashraf ko designs dene lagee…

We pull out from a design

MIRA: VO

Ek dinn jab mein Ashraf ke paas pahunchee to usnay kaha…

ASHRAF

Tumhaare paas kya yahee ek kapde hain…

Mira looks at Ashraf

ASHRAF

Last time bhi tum yahee pahne thee… lo ye dress le lo…

Mira looks at Ashraf

ASHRAF

Rakh lo… tum per achchee lagegi… try kar lo…

Mira tries the dress in the trial room

MIRA: VO

Dress ko dekhnay ke baad Ashraf ne mujhse kaha…

ASHRAF

Ah… bas thodi fitting sahee karnee hai…

Mira stands as Ashraf bends on his knees and adjusts the dress and then he touches her in a suggestive manner.

MIRA: VO

Dress ko theek karte karte Ashraf ne mujhe galat tareekay se chua…

MIRA

Ashraf…

ASHRAF

Kisi ko kuch pata nahin chalega… tum bhi musalmaan mein bhi musalmaan… sab theek ho jaayega…

Mira looks at Ashraf in a very angry manner

MIRA: VO

Uss dinn mujhe laga… ki shaayad iss duniya mein… har paraaya aadmi har paraayee aurat ko ek hee tareekay se dekhta hai… aur mujhe aadmiyon se nafrat ho gayee…

Scene – 26

Look of Nirbhay

NIRBHAY

Toh aadmiyon se nafrat karnay waali Mira... ek aadmi ko apnee virginity neelaam karnay waali Virgin Mira kaise bann gayee?

Mira is hurt at Nirbhay's comment

MIRA

You are hurting me...

NIRBHAY

Sorry... journalist hoon naa... nikal gaya...

Mira heaves heavily... she is tense... nirbhay sees it... he offers her a glass of water...

NIRBHAY

Thoda paani pee lo...

Mira drinks from the glass

MIRA

Thanks...

Just then there is an audio overlap – **"milnay ka waqt khatm ho chukka hai..."**

Nirbhay sighs he gets up & leaves. He turns as he reaches the door & looks towards Mira

MIRA

Burger lete aana... *nirbhay smiles...* aur kya mujhe naye kapday mil saktay hain...

NIRBHAY *smiles*

Of course… take care…

He closes the door

Cut to

Scene – 27

We pull out from the tight close up of Nirbhay, he is looking at someone transfixed, we reveal it's a night club

Cut of Mira moving wildly on the dance floor to the music

Just then Nisha comes with drinks to Nirbhay. She sees that Nirbhay is a bit lost

NISHA

Kya hua Nirbhay aren't you enjoying…

NIRBHAY

No… I am enjoying…

NISHA *as if she has caught him*

NIRBHAY… mein tumhein bahut achche se jaanti hoon… tum Mira ke bare mein soch rahay ho naa…

Nirbhay looks at Nisha and then he smiles… and nods…

NISHA

Bachke rehna…

Dissolve to

Scene – 28

Top /_ shot. Mira is sitting with Nirbhay sitting across, staring at her.

MIRA

Kya hua?

NIRBHAY

Kuch nahin… bas aisay hee…

MIRA

Pooch taach badee boring hoti hai naa?

NIRBHAY

Hmmm… smiles… except for the leg crossing scene in Basic Instinct…

Mira smiles

MIRA

Vaise ye scene mujhe seedha Basic Instinct ke jaisa lag raha hai…

Look of Nirbhay

Mira opens her legs.

Nirbhay sighs.

NIRBHAY

Ye scene Basic Instinct ke jaisa issliye nahin ho sakta kyunki naa to tum Sharon Stone ho aur naa hee mein Michael Douglus… aur naa hee tumhaare haath mein cigarette hai…

MIRA

Hmmm… aur sabse badee baat… I am wearing my undies…

Look of Nirbhay

Mira smiles

Nirbhay too, smiles

Mira walks upto Nirbhay with a sexy swagger

MIRA

Per ek cheez hai… she comes very close to nirbhay… kahin tum mere saath Basic Instinct kee tarah involve mat ho jaana…

A look of lust in the eyes of both… and after a pregnant pause, she kisses nirbhay.

He responds… they both get physical…

NIRBHAY *pulling back*

WAIT… *takes a deep breath*... wait… wait… wait… *Mira looks at Nirbhay... nirbhay looks at her*... Dekho… I am on duty… control… abhi mein ye sab nahin kar sakta hoon…

MIRA

To kab kar saktay ho ye sab…

Nirbhay sighs

Look of Mira

Look of Nirbhay

Mira jumps on Nirbhay.

Nirbhay and Mira bang on the door

Outside

The cop sees at the door banging. He frowns and he looks at a lady cop.

She too looks at the door.

She then looks at the cop.

She smiles.

The cop gets up & opens his belt.

The lady cop also gets up as she unbuttons the topmost button of her shirt and closes her eyes.

Fade to black

Scene – 29

Mira is sitting smoking a cigarette.
Nirbhay sits across staring at her.

MIRA

Kya hua?

NIRBHAY

Soch raha hoon… should I do it?

MIRA

Itna socho mat… I am ready… pasand ho tum mujhe…

Look of Nirbhay

… OK… whenever you are ready

Mira smiles

NIRBHAY

Aagay kya hua?

MIRA

Jaisa ki maine bataaya… mere abbu ka sapna thaa ki mein padh-likh kar kuch banoon… unkay jaane ke baad… aur Rahul aur Ashraf ke saath huye apnay experience ke baad maine paaya ki zindagi kitni mushkil hai…

Continues her story

Scene – 30

Night. Mira looks at the bakery teary eyed

MIRA: VO

Bakery ko bhi bakery maalik ne mujhse khaali karva liya… ab mere paas kuch bhi nahin bacha thaa..

Scene – 31

Mira telling her story

MIRA

Kyunki Rahul aur Ashraf ne ab meri madad karnee band kar dee thee… issliye mere paise bhi dheeray dheeray khatm ho rahay thay…

Mein toot rahee thee… naa khaane ko paisa… naa rehnay ko rupya… aisay mein ek dinn Rahul ka dobaara se mujhe phone aaya… he wanted to sleep with me…

Rahul ka phone aanay ke baad… mein bahut pareshaan thee… ki mein kya karoon… ki meri nazar ek newspaper article per padee… ussmein mere jaisee hee ek ladki ki kahaani thee… jo ki London mein rehtee thee… aur apnee padhaayee ko jaari rakhnay ke liye… usnay apnee virginity auction kar dee thee…

Look of Nirbhay

NIRBHAY

Kya ye kaam prostitution jaisa nahin hua?

MIRA

Nahin… kyunki uss ladki ke mutaabik… aajkal ke zamaane mein jab ladkiyaan are ready to do anything…

Look of Nirbhay

VIRGINITY ek premium tissue hai… aur usee tissue kee vajah se usay paise mil rahay thay… uske mutaabik vo apnee body nahin… balki apna tissue bech rahee thee…

Look of Nirbhay

Uss article ko padhnay ke baad mujhe ekdum se Rahul aur Ashraf kee baat dhyaan mein aa gayee… aakhir vo bhi toh mujhse yahee chahte thay? Aur maine socha… kee jab mere paas premium tissue hai… to mein apna shareer kyun bechoon, balki apna premium tissue kyun naa bechoon… aur maine decide kar liya ki mein apnee virginity ko internet per auction karoongi…

Look of Nirbhay
Look of Mira

Ad dete waqt hee mujhe lag gaya thaa… ki mera ad hit hoga… kyunki jis webcaster se maine ad design karvaayee uskee aankhon mein maine apne liye ek… desire see dekhi… ek aag see dekhi…

Dissolve to

Scene – 32

Visual: ladies burning copies of newspaper in front of mira's building. Banners denouncing Mira. Mira peeps out of the window

MIRA: VO

Ek aur aag bhi maine dekhi… hamare desh kee moral police… alag alag mahila sansthaanon ne mere ghar ke aage pradarshan karnay shuru kar diye…

SUBHASHINI

Mira ko baahar nikaalo… Mira ko baahar nikaalo…

Dissolve to

Mira comes out

SUBHASHINI

Tumhein sharm nahin aati… apnee virginity ko bechtay huye… khulay aam prostitution kartay huye…

Visual: Mira ushers ladies in the hall

MIRA: VO

Unn ladies kee representatives ko maine apnay yahan bulaaya…

The ladies sit… Mira speaks as she sits

MIRA starts tentatively, struggles to find the right words but gains command with the graph of the dialogue

Aunty… kisi bhi ladkee ke liye virginity ek aisa issue hota hai… joki kaafi sensitive hota hai… chahe vo India ho ya abroad… aisay mein… agar koyee ladki… apnee virginity ko bechnay… auction karnay ka ad nikaalti hai… to its natural… kee uskee kuch bahut badee majboori yaa majbooriyaan rahee hongi… kya aapne jaannay kee koshish kee… ki mein apnee virginity kyun bech raheen hoon?

Ladies look at each other…

SUBHASHINI

Kyun?

MIRA

Jissay ki aagay chalkar mein vaqayee mein prostitute naa bann jaaoon… A bang, all ladies look at each other… kya aapne kabhi, bhookhay pet raat guzzari hai, trash bin mein se khaana nikaalkar khaaya hai… A bang, all ladies look at each other… per mujhe to inn aam zarooraton ke alaava… ek khwaab bhi poora karna hai… padhne ka khwaab… mujhe rupaye chahiye… apnay aapko establish karnay ke liye hee mein itna bada kadam utha rahee hoon…

SUBHASHINI

Lekin paisa kamaane ke aur bhi tareekay hain!

MIRA

Mujh jaisi ladki ke liye kya tareekay hain… zara bataaiye…

Subhashini look at the other ladies

Mere abbu aur ammi ke marne ke baad mera ek khaas dost bana thaa Rahul… sarcastically... padayee ke liye rupaye dene ke bahaane vo mujhe use karna chahta thaa… {cuts of Rahul's story} aur meri ammi ke client Ashraf saab ka bhi iraada yahee thaa… {cuts of Ashraf's story}

Subhashini look at the other ladies…

SUBHASHINI

Koyee scholarship vagairah…

MIRA

Try kiya thaa… per badkismati se… mein kahin per bhi scholarship ke liye qualify nahin kar paayee…

Subhashini look at the other ladies…

MIRA

Achcha aap hee mujhe bataaiye… aapke organisation mein kitni auratein hain…

SUBHASHINI

Ek hazaar…

MIRA

Ek hazaar… Mira looks at Subhashini… kya aap ya aapki organization mujhe support karegi… aapki organisation kee har aurat ko… sirf ek hazaar rupaye contribute karke mujhe dene hain… taaki mein… apnay aap ko establish kar sakoon…

Subhashini look at other ladies

ONE LADY

Mujhe to apnee beti kee shaadi ke liye ek ek rupya bachaana hai…

Subhashini looks at Mira

SUBHASHINI

Hum tumhein thoday bahut rupaye de sakte hain…

MIRA

Thoday bahut rupyon se meri padhayee to poori nahin hogi naa… aur jab vo rupaye khatm ho jaayengay… tab mein kya karoongi?

Subhashini looks at Mira

Aunty… aisay bahut se issues hain… jo ki mere iss tissue se jyaada zaroori hain… jinnko ki aapki organisation ko address karna chahiye…

Visual: the ladies get up and leave they are feeling rather helpless

MIRA: VO

Mere logic ke aage vo auratein chup ho gayeen aur chalee gayeen…

Cut to

Scene – 33

We show everyone is listening to Mira with rapt attention

NIRBHAY

Jab tumhaara ad internet per aaya… to tumhein kaisa response mila…

MIRA

Teen dinon ke ander ander hee… mere ad per lagbhag thirty thousand hits huye thay…

NIRBHAY

Just shows… that sex sells…

MIRA

I would say… VIRGINITY sells…

Nirbhay smiles

NIRBHAY

MIRA… tum ek musalmaan ho… tumhaare mazhab mein Sania Mirza kee skirt ke ooper bhi fatwa jaari kar diya jaata hai… tumhaare iss faislay per bhi bawaal utha thaa…

MIRA

Bawaal… chaaron taraf aag hee aag thee… mujhe yaad hai… mujhe kaafir karaar de diya gaya thaa… per tum mujhe bataao ki kya agar koyee ladki izzat ke saath jeena chahti hai to vo gunaah hai… aatankwaadiyon ko… underworld dons ko… jo ki begunaahon ko maarte hain… zulm karte hain… unnko musalmaan maana jaata hai… islam ka rehnuma maana jaata hai…

Look of Nirbhay

Maaf karna… quran shareef ye seekh nahin deti hai… jo bomb blasts hotay hain… kya unnmein musalmaan nahin marte hain… MARTE HAIN… aur quran kisi bhi insaan kee jaan lene kee ijaazat nahin deti hai… MEIN TOH maanti hoon ki iss jahaan mein ek umdaa insaan ko hee musalmaan kehlaane ka haq hota hai aur mera allah jaanta hai ki mein ek umda insaan hoon… ab koyee mujhe maarne ka fatwa jaari kar de… toh uskee zid… per mein maanti hoon ki allah kee marzi ke bagair patta bhi nahin hil sakta…

Nirbhay looks at her intently

NIRBHAY

Aagay kya hua…

MIRA

Mein apnee virginity kisi tom, dick ya harry ko nahin dena chahti thee… issliye maine saare profiles ko bahut hee achche se study kiya aur poora time liya… aakhir mujhe Raghav Krishna ka profile pasand aa gaya… uske kuch business interests thay… aur vo kisi zamaane mein maana hua jewelry designer bhi thaa… ab vo retire ho chuka thaa… mein jaanti thee ki Raghav aagay bhi meri madad kar sakta hai…

NIRBHAY

Hmmm… jab tum pehli baar Raghav se mili to tumhein kaisa laga?

Mira listens to Nirbhay’s question and closes her eyes

Cut to

Scene – 34

Close on: Champagne flowing out of the bottle.
As we pull out we see in soft focus Mira is standing wearing a burqa, her face is covered with naqab
Raghav (his face is not visible) turns with champagne bottle in his hand

RAGHAV

Champagne…

MIRA

Mein sharaab nahin peeti…

RAGHAV

Good… sehat ke liye… takes a sip… jyaada achchi nahin hoti…
Look of Mira

RAGHAV

Tumhaare account mein rupaye transfer ho gaye?

MIRA

Mujhe aap per bharosa hai…

RAGHAV

Kabhi bhi… kisi per bharosa nahin karna chahiye…

MIRA

Phir aapne mujhper bharosa kyun kiya?
Raghav looks at Mira

MIRA

Ho sakta hai mein VIRGIN naa houun… she throws off her burqa…

Mira stands cinematically nude in front of Raghav

Raghav looks at Mira – we reveal Raghav's face for the first time, he looks at Mira with desire in his eyes

He walks upto Mira and picks up the burqa and covers her up

RAGHAV

Nahin abhi nahin…

MIRA

Sir please… aapko jo karna hai vo jaldi kijiye… mein yahan se jald se jald vaapas jaaker… apnee aagay kee zindagi jeena chahti hoon… apnee padayee poori karna chahti hoon…

Look of Raghav to Mira

Look of Mira

RAGHAV

Cold drink logi…

MIRA

Nahin…

RAGHAV

Mira… mere paas sabkuch hai… rupya, paisa, aisho-aaraam… har sukh… per mere paas koyee company nahin hai… mein tumse sirf company chahta hoon…

MIRA

Matlab?

RAGHAV

Simple… mein chahta hoon ki tum mere saath yahan per raho… mujhe company do… that's it…

MIRA

And SEX…

RAGHAV

Nahin… mein tumse koyee sex nahin chahta hoon…

Mira looks at Raghav a bit perplexed

MIRA

Tumnay sirf company dene ke liye… mujhe itna rupya diya…

Raghav nods in yes

MIRA

Tum paagal ho…

Charge on Mira

Scene – 35

We pull out of Mira's face as Nirbhay interrupts her

NIRBHAY

Hey… hang on… ab mein pagal ho jaaoonga… tumhaare kehnay ka matlab hai… ki Raghav ne sirf company dene ke liye tumhein itna rupya de diya…

MIRA

Haan…

NIRBHAY

You mean to say you are virgin?

MIRA

Maine aisa to nahin kaha…

Look of Nirbhay

NIRBHAY

Meri to kuch samajh mein nahin aa raha hai…
Audio overlap: milnay ka waqt khatm hua

MIRA

Ufff…

NIRBHAY

Don't worry… der se hee sahee but we are through with this…

Look of Mira

… maine tumhaari bail arrange karva dee hai… kal hum yahan per nahin balki mere flat per milengay…

Mira looks at Nirbhay

MIRA

Some light at last…

Look of Nirbhay

… ek ghanay andhere ke baad…

Mira closes her eyes

Fade to black

I N T E R V A L

Scene – 36

Exterior shot of Nirbhay's building

Dissolve to

We dissolve to Nirbhay's flat

NIRBHAY a bit tentatively

So Raghav… tumhaare saath sirf… WAQT bitaana chahta thaa… per tumnay abhi abhi kaha ki tum virgin nahin ho… so…

MIRA

Meri kahaani khatm hotay hotay tumhein sab pata chal jaayega…

Look of Nirbhay

Charge on Mira

Scene – 37

Raghav chahta thaa ki mein garmiyaan uske saath bitaaoon… kyunki uska chhota bhai apnee family ke saath aane waala thaa… jab maine Raghav se apnee padaaye ke baare mein kaha to usnay kaha ki padayee cheh maheenay late shuru kar lena… usnay mujhse kaha ki vo mujhe ek American university mein sponsorship de dega… American University kee baat sunnkar mein chup ho gayee…

We pull out from Mira's face

MIRA

Promise…

RAGHAV

Gentleman's promise…

Mira smiles

RAGHAV

Come I will show you the house…

Visual: Raghav plays the old gramophone

MIRA: VO

Raghav mein ek authority thee… joki kisi bhi ladkee ko uskee taraf kheenchtee thee… after a pause… shaayad…

Dissolve to

Scene – 38

Visual: Raghav gets Mira to the breakfast table

MIRA: VO

Raghav stylish bhi thaa… uske saath meri pehli subah bahut hee special thee… usnay waterfall ke aagay breakfast set karvaaya thaa…

RAGHAV

Kaisa lag raha hai…

MIRA

Achcha…

RAGHAV

Ekdum ek princess ke jaisa…

Mira smiles

RAGHAV

You have got a beautiful smile…

MIRA

Thanks…

RAGHAV

Aur ek baat boloon…

MIRA

Hmmm…

RAGHAV

Gussay mein tum ekdum TIGRESS ke jaisee lagtee hogi…

MIRA

Tigress… how can you say that?

RAGHAV

Gyaan… ladkiyon ka kaafi gyaan hai mujhe…

MIRA

Hmmm… kitni ladkiyaan theen tumhaari life mein…

Visual: Raghav looks at Mira and smiles

Visual: Mira eats while maintaining eye contact with Raghav

MIRA: VO

Raghav ke saath rehkar meri life completely change ho gayee… something similar to my life in Bahrain…

Scene – 39

Raghav is praying, Mira comes and looks at Raghav

RAGHAV

Aao bhagwaan ko haath jodh lo…

MIRA

Mein…

RAGHAV

Hindu musalmaan to humnay banaaya hai… usnay to humein sirf insaan banaaya hai… chaaho to namaaz padh lo…

Mira smiles and comes in. She folds her hands and prays
Raghav looks at Mira praying
As Mira turns towards Raghav, Raghav says

RAGHAV

Tumhaara naam Mira kaise pada… Mira to hindu naam hota hai naa…

MIRA

Abhi abhi to tumnay kaha thaa ki hindu musalmaan to humnay banaaya hai… usnay to humein sirf insaan banaaya hai…

Look of Raghav

Insaan hoon issliye mera naam MIRA hai… shaayad…

Vaise school mein pada thaa… ki Mira… Krishna bhagwaan kee bhakt theen… aur ye bhi pada thaa ki vo aajeevan kunwaari rahee theen…

RAGHAV

Yeah… virgin… like you…

Look of Mira
Look of Raghav

Scene – 40

Visual: Raghav is making a painting of Mira

MIRA: VO

Dheeray dheeray mein aur Raghav kareeb aate chalay gaye…

Raghav shows the painting to Mira

RAGHAV

Come… kaisi lagee…

MIRA

Oh… it's wonderful… kaafi creative ho tum…

RAGHAV

Haan vo to mein hoon… vaise tum bhi kaafi creative ho…

MIRA

How can you say that?

RAGHAV

Gyaan… ladkiyon ka kaafi gyaan hai mujhe…

MIRA

Hmmm… kitni ladkiyaan theen tumhaari life mein…

Raghav looks at Mira and smiles
Mira maintains an eye contact with Raghav

Scene – 41

Visual: Mira showing her designs to Raghav

MIRA: VO

Ek dinn maine Raghav ko apnay jewelry ke designs dikhaaye…

RAGHAV

Achchay design banaati ho… mera ek store hai… why don't you look after it… loss mein jaa raha hai… ho sakta hai tumhaare jaane ke baad faayda ho jaaye…

Scene – 42

Visual: Raghav and Mira in the store

MIRA: VO

Aur maine Raghav ka store bahut hee achche se sambhaal liya…

RAGHAV

Khush lag rahee ho…

MIRA

Hmmm…

RAGHAV

Vaise ek baat boloon… mujhe lagta hai ki ab tum padh-likh kar kya karogi… tum iss store ko hee sambhaal lo… I will pay you well…

MIRA

Nahin… mere abbu ka ek sapna thaa… jo ki mujhe poora karna hai…

Look of Raghav to Mira
Look of Mira to Raghav

RAGHAV

Haan ye baat to tumnay sahee kahee… humein apnay badon ka sapna zaroor poora karna chahiye… per mere khyaal se tumhaare abbu chahte hongay ki padh-likh kar tum apnay pairon per khadee ho… kamaao… iss store se tum kamaaogi… to ek tarah se unka sapna bhi poora ho jaayega… aur tum bhi khush rahogi…

MIRA

How can you say that?

RAGHAV

Gyaan… ladkiyon ka kaafi gyaan hai mujhe…

MIRA

Hmmm… kitni ladkiyaan theen tumhaari life mein…

Raghav looks at Mira and smiles

MIRA

Your smile is not gonna work this time around… kitni ladkiyaan theen tumhaari life mein…

Scene – 43

Visual: Mira is flipping through a photo album

MIRA: VO

Raghav ne mujhe ek photo album dee… jissmein uskee life mein aayee ladkiyon kee photos theen…

Mira looks at Raghav

Raghav looks at Mira

MIRA

Raghav issmein to bas ek hee ladkee kee photo hain…

Raghav, his eyes have moistened up, nods in yes

RAGHAV

Meri life mein bas ek hee ladki thee… Angel kehta thaa mein usay… Christian thee…

MIRA

Kya hua…

RAGHAV

Kya hua… hmmm… yahee to tragedy hai ki kuch hua hee nahin…

MIRA

Marr gayee…

RAGHAV

Ahnnn… uska ek ex-boyfriend thaa… ye uske saath patch up karna chahti thee… per tabtak mein Angel se bahut pyar karnay lag gaya thaa… maine issay kaha – tumhaare bagair mein jee nahin paaoonga… koyee farak hee nahin pada usay… uthee aur chali gayee…

Raghav looks at Mira with deep hurt in his eyes

MIRA

Per uske baad aur ladkiyaan…

RAGHAV

Kayeeyon ne try kiya… per I just couldn't trust any one of them…

MIRA

And me…

RAGHAV

I trust you…

MIRA

How can you say that?

RAGHAV

Gyaan… ladkiyon ka kaafi gyaan hai mujhe…

Mira smiles and looks in Raghav's eyes

Scene – 44

Visual: Raghav is reading out from a book to Mira

MIRA: VO

Jaise jaise mein raghav ko kareeb se jaanti gayee… mera interest ussmein badhta gaya…

RAGHAV

Tumhaara dhyaan meri taraf nahin hai…

MIRA

How can you say that?

RAGHAV

Gyaan… ladkiyon ka kaafi gyaan hai mujhe…

Mira gets up and crawls upto Raghav

MIRA

Kiss me…

Raghav looks at Mira smile vanishes from his face

MIRA

Kiss me…

RAGHAV with a troubled face

No I can't…

MIRA

But why?

Raghav looks at Mira for a while

RAGHAV

Ye baat tum kisi ko bataaogi nahin... till the time I die…

MIRA

Raghav…

RAGHAV

Angel se break-up ke baad… mujhe apne jeenay ka koyee maqsad nahin dikhta thaa… issliye I drove down to commit suicide… kismet… teen maheenay coma mein rehnay ke baad bhi bach gaya… per doctors ne mujhe bataaya… that I won't be able to…

Mira looks at Raghav…
Raghav looks at Mira
Mira gently kisses Raghav on his cheek

Cut to

Scene – 45

Exterior shot of the nirbhay's flat

Dissolve to

We dissolve to the nirbhay's flat
NIRBHAY with great surprise

Raghav Krishan was not medically fit… phir aakhir Raghav ne tumhaara bid offer kyun accept kiya…

MIRA

Maine bhi yahee baat Raghav se poochi…

Scene – 46 SCENE 44 CONT'D

Visual: Raghav and Mira are sitting on the bed

MIRA: VO

Raghav ne mujhse kaha… ki vo ek tanha akeli zindagi jee raha thaa… jab internet per usnay mera ad dekha… to vo samajh gaya ki mein bhi usee kee tarah tanha akeli hoon… usay laga ki ek tanha akeli ladki hee uskee tanhaayee, uske akelepan ka dard samajh paayegi… issliye usnay mujhe approach kiya…

Raghav looks at Mira
Mira looks at Raghav

RAGHAV

Aisa nahin hai ki iss tanhaayee ko mitaane ke liye maine pahle kabhi kisi ko approach naa kiya ho… per jo bhi ladkee tumhaare se pahle aayee… vo dhokhebaaz hee nikli, Angel kee tarah… kisi ko rupyaa chahiye thaa to kisi ko heeray-jawaharaat… har baar dhokha khaane ke baad mein samajh nahin paa raha thaa ki mein kya karoon… ki maine tumhaara ad dekha… aur bas mujhe pata chal gaya ki tumheen mere dard ki dava ho…

Look of Mira to Raghav
Look of Raghav to Mira

Fade to black

Scene – 47

Exterior shot of the nirbhay's building

Dissolve to

We dissolve to the nirbhay's flat

MIRA

Aur uss dinn Raghav aur mere beech… ek ekdum naya bond… ek naya rishta develop ho gaya…

Look of Nirbhay
Look of Mira

Dissolve to

Scene – 48

Visual: Breakfast table is laid. Raghav and Mira are sitting over there

MIRA: VO

Ek subah Raghav ne mujhe bataaya ki uska bhai aur bhateeja… ussay milnay ke liye aa rahay hain…

Raghav ne mujhe apnee family se introduce karvaaya… Viki – uska bhai aur Brad uska bhateeja…

Viki se milte waqt mujhe intuition hua… ki vo mujhse milkar khush nahin hai…

Scene – 49

Visual: Raghav and Viki fighting. Mira is listening to them, she is hiding

MIRA: VO

Mera intuition sahee thaa… kyunki raat mein maine Viki ko Raghav ke saath ladhte huye dekha…

VIKI

Mira ko apnay saath rakhnay ka matlab?

Look of Raghav to Viki

RAGHAV

Akela thaa mein… maine tumse kaha to thaa ki mere paas aaker raho… per tum… tumhein toh shaher mein rehna hai… apnay akelepan ko door karne ke liye hee maine Mira ko bulaaya hai… aur phir mein jaanta hoon ki maine kuch galat nahin kiya hai…

VIKI

Duniya to nahin jaanti naa… tarah tarah kee baatein kar rahay hain log…

RAGHAV

Logon ka kaam hota hai… baatein karna…

Look of Viki to Raghav
Look of Raghav to Viki

VIKI

Maine suna hai ki jewelery store ka saara kaam, Mira hee sambhaal rahee hai… jewelry store ko lekar aapka iraada kya hai?

Raghav looks at Viki for a while
Look of Viki to Raghav

RAGHAV

Kal janmaashtmi hai… subah jaldi uthna hai… so jaao…

Look of Viki to Raghav
Look of Raghav to Viki

Scene – 50

Visual: Raghav in temple, Mira comes dressed in saffron

MIRA: VO

Janmaashtmi ke dinn Raghav aur Viki kee tensions aur badh gayeen…

RAGHAV

Aaj to tum vaqayee mein Mira lag rahee ho…

MIRA

Jaante ho main iss tarah se kyun taiyaar huyee hoon?

RAGHAV

Koyee khaas vajah hee hogi…

MIRA

How can you say that?

RAGHAV

Gyaan… ladkiyon ka kaafi gyaan hai mujhe…

MIRA

Hmmm…

Raghav looks at Mira and smiles

MIRA

Kal raat ko mein ek TV channel dekh rahee thee… ussmein bataaya gaya ki Raghav… Krishna bhagwaan ke anek naamon mein se… unheen ka ek naam hai…

RAGHAV

Hmmm…

MIRA

Issliye mein iss tarah se taiyaar huyee hoon…

Raghav smiles
Just then Viki and Brad come
Raghav immediately picks up Brad

RAGHAV

Hey mera Kanhaiya… Mira… mera Kanhaiya cute lagta hai naa?

MIRA

Haan…

Mira squeezes Brad's cheeks
Viki gives an angry look to Mira

VIKI

Stop doing that…

Look of Brad to Viki

Flashcut: Pooja
Flashcut: Aarti
Flashcut: Raghav offers aarti to Mira
Visual: As Mira takes the aarti, an infuriated Viki leaves
Visual: Raghav looks at Viki leaving

MIRA: VO

Viki ko ye baat achchee nahin lagee ki Raghav ne Viki se pahle mere ko aarti dee…

Scene – 51

Visual: Viki leaving in the car

MIRA: VO

Uske baad Viki ek pal ke liye bhi vahan per nahin ruka… shaam ko hee vo vaapaas jaane laga… Brad chahta thaa ki vo Raghav ke paas rukay… aur Raghav bhi yahee chahta thaa…

Raghav nods in yes
The car leaves
Raghav stands with Mira and Brad
Raghav and Mira are looking at the car leaving
Brad is looking at Mira

Scene – 52

Visual: Mira is working on the lap-top. Brad comes in

MIRA: VO

Brad ko, mere saath kiya gaya Viki ka behaviour achcha nahin laga…

BRAD

I am sorry about my dad's behaviour…

MIRA

It's ok…

BRAD

Kya kar rahee ho tum?

MIRA

Apnee padhayee ke liye universities dekh rahee hoon…

BRAD

Padh-likh kar tum kya karogi?

MIRA

Apnay abbu ka khwaab poora karoongi…

BRAD

Tum jaanti ho meri class mein ek ladki hai… I like her… per vo kehti hai ki vo padhna chahti hai…

MIRA

Ok…

BRAD

Pata nahin… saari ladkiyaan padhna kyun chahti hain?

Mira look at Brad and smiles

Scene – 53

Visual: Brad is doing something on the dining table. Mira comes over

MIRA: VO

Jaldi hee mere aur Brad ke beech mein ek bond develop honay laga…

MIRA

Brad…

Brad signals her to keep quiet
Mira wonders as if what is Brad doing
She walks upto him
She looks that Brad is making a sign
CUTS: Brad is making a danger sign

MIRA

Why are you making this ghastly sign?

Brad signals her to keep quiet

Brad continues making the sign

As Brad finishes he looks up

MIRA

Why?

BRAD

Cos there is danger ahead…

MIRA

Danger… what danger?

Brad farts

MIRA

Oh shit…

BRAD with a devilish grin

See I told you…

Look of Mira to Brad

BRAD

Ek baat boloon…

MIRA

Hmmm…

BRAD

Gussay mein tum ekdum TIGRESS ke jaisee lagtee hogi…

Mira looks at Brad, she can see reflection of Raghav in him

Charge on Mira

Scene – 54

Visual: Mira is sleeping, she wakes up as she finds someone caressing her head, she wakes up

MIRA

Brad…

BRAD

Mujhe akele sotay huye darr lagta hai…

Mira looks at Brad

BRAD

Kya mein tumhaare saath so jaaoon…

Mira looks at Brad

Brad climbs up the bed and closes his eyes

Mira looks at Brad and closes her eyes

Brad turns towards Mira and hugs her tight

Mira opens her eyes

Scene – 55

Visual: Brad is on the bed with his eyes closed, Mira comes out of the loo, she is drying her hair with towel

BRAD

Mira… can I ask you something?

Mira looks at Brad

BRAD

Am I hot?

Mira looks at Brad and then she controls her laughter

BRAD

Issmein hansne kee kya baat hai?

MIRA

Tumse kisnay kaha ki tum hot ho?

BRAD

It's obvious… mera naam Brad hai… aur Brad naam ke saare log hot hotay hain…

Mira looks at Brad in a blank manner

BRAD

Brad Pitt…

MIRA

Tumhaari baatein jo hai naa… vo badee strange hain…

BRAD

Tum bhi to badee strange ho…

MIRA

Matlab?

BRAD

You are my tau's girlfriend…

MIRA

Who told you that?

BRAD

My father…

MIRA

Unhonay tumhein bataaya…

BRAD

Nahin mom ko bata rahay thay… maine bhi sunn liya…

Mira looks at Brad

BRAD

Tumnay mere tau ki girlfriend bannay ke liye unsay rupaye bhi liye hain… issliye to meri mom tumse milnay ke liye nahin aayeen…

Look of Brad to Mira

Look of Mira to Brad

MIRA

Tum abhi bahut chhote ho… kuch baatein abhi tumhaari samajh mein nahin aayengi…

BRAD

Mein chhota nahin hoon… mein bada ho gaya hoon… mein toh ye bhi jaanta hoon ki mujhe kya banna hai… ek painter…

MIRA

Good…

BRAD

Will you pose for me?

Mira throws the towel at Brad
Brad looks at Mira

Scene – 56

Mira is sitting silent, her eyes are moist

MIRA

Bahut miss kartee hoon mein Raghav ko…

Nirbhay looks at her…

MIRA

Nirbhay… mera mood kharaab ho gaya hai… kuch aur baatein karein…

Nirbhay looks at her…

NIRBHAY

Kuch aur baatein matlab?

MIRA

Kuch apnay bare mein bataao… apnee girlfriends ke baare mein…

Look of Nirbhay to Mira
Look of Mira to Nirbhay

MIRA

Bataao naa…

NIRBHAY *after a good look to her*

Jab mein 12th class mein thaa… to mere saamne waale flat mein ek bahut hee raabchik item aayee thee… she was sex… ek dinn usnay apna introduction mujhe diya… charge on Nirbhay… aur kaha ki vo iss shaher mein nayee hai can I show her around… so I showed her around…

Look of Mira to Nirbhay

MIRA

Phir kya hua?

NIRBHAY

Hona kya thaa… mein serious ho gaya… VO masti chahti thee… BAS... but it taught me a very important lesson… kabhi bhi kisi ladki ke bare mein serious mat hona…

Mira looks at Nirbhay

MIRA

Kya VAQAYEE ab tum kabhi bhi kisi bhi ladki ke baare mein serious nahin hogay…

Nirbhay looks at Mira with surprise
Mira gives a meaningful look to Nirbhay
Nirbhay looks at Mira

MIRA comes close to Nirbhay and looks in his eyes intently

Are you still not ready?

Nirbhay looks at Mira
Mira kisses him…
Within a fraction of a second, Nirbhay goes totally wild… he is feeling Mira rather hungrily and roughly…
He is all over her… Mira too is responding in a very loud manner… in a matter of seconds they are totally wild
They pant for breath looking at each other

Lead in to SONG 2

SONG 2

Scene – 57

Nirbhay is making notes on computer.
Mira comes to him with coffee
Nirbhay smiles and as he takes coffee, he takes a sip
Mira settles down

NIRBHAY

Tumhaari iss poori story mein… ek cheez mujhe samajh mein nahin aa rahee hai…

Look of Mira

Tumnay mujhse kaha thaa ki Raghav was not medically fit… aur uskay fauran baad tumnay ye bhi kaha thaa ki you are not Virgin… can you explain it?

MIRA: VO

Actually Raghav ke saath kahin naa kahin… mein ek emotional tareekay se involve ho gayee thee…

Scene – 58

Visual: Mira and Brad are lying on the bed

BRAD

Mira…

MIRA

Hmmm…

BRAD

Do you love my tau?

Mira looks at Brad

MIRA

Do you love your tau?

BRAD

Yes I do… what about you?

MIRA

Yes I do…

Charge on Mira's face

Scene – 59

Visual: Raghav is reading a book, Mira comes in… Raghav looks at Mira

MIRA

Raghav… I think… I love you…

RAGHAV

Mira… that's just a stupid thought… tum jaanti ho ye possible nahin hai…

MIRA

Why… because of your accident…

Raghav nods in a yes

MIRA

Raghav… meri ek dost ne mujhe bataaya thaa… ki ek aurat ke liye do tarah ke orgasms hotay hain… Physical Orgasm aur Emotional Orgasm… physical orgasm ek myth hai… emotional orgasm ek reality… and you don't have to be physically fit to give me an emotional orgasm…

Raghav looks at Mira
Mira looks at Raghav

RAGHAV

Mira per…

MIRA

Raghav mujhe nahin pata hai ki mein sahee kar rahee hoon ya galat… but I think I love you…

She kisses Raghav gently
Raghav looks at Mira
Mira looks at Raghav
Music leads in

Scene – 60

Exterior shot of the nirbhay's flat

Dissolve to

We dissolve to the nirbhay's flat floor

MIRA

Nirbhay… ho sakta hai ki uss waqt mein technically Virgin hounn… per mujhe lagta hai ki ek aurat Orgasm experience karnay ke baad, virginity loose kar deti hai… Raghav se milay uss Emotional Orgasm ke baad mujhe laga… ki… I wasn't virgin anymore…

Silence for a few seconds

NIRBHAY

Mira inn sab happenings ke beech aakhir vo kya haalaat thay… jinnkay chalte Raghav ka murder hua…

Scene – 61

Visual: Raghav is spraying water on the leaves

MIRA: VO

Garmiyaan beet chuki theen… sardiyaan aane waalin theen… ek dinn mein Raghav ke paas gayee…

MIRA

Raghav… mere khyaal se ab mujhe chalna chahiye…

Raghav looks at Mira for a while

RAGHAV

Kahan jaana chahti ho tum?

MIRA

Apnee padhaayee poori karne ke liye…

RAGHAV

Mere ko tanha akela chhodkar…

Look of Mira to Raghav

Look of Raghav

RAGHAV

Thoday dinn aur thehar jaao…

MIRA

Per… iss tarah se to poora ek saal nikal jaayega…

RAGHAV

Padhaayee to tum kabhi bhi shuru kar saktee ho… per ho sakta hai ki mera saath bas saal do saal ka aur ho…

MIRA

Raghav…

RAGHAV

I have got some other plans for you… come…

Raghav gives some papers to Mira…

MIRA

Ye kya hain Raghav?

RAGHAV

Store ke papers… maine store tumhaare naam kar diya hai…

Mira looks at Raghav

MIRA

Raghav…

RAGHAV

It's natural… vo store mere liye dead business thaa… losses mein jaa raha thaa… tumnay mujhe uss store se faayda karvaaya… that proves you can run the store…

MIRA

Per meri padhaayee…

RAGHAV

Store tumhaara ho chukka hai… achche khaase rupaye kamaaogi… kya ab bhi tumhein padayee kee zaroorat hai?

Look of Mira to Raghav
Charge on Mira
Mira closes her eyes

Fade to black

Scene – 62

Visual: Mira in jewelery store
Visual: Subhashini comes to the jewelery store

MIRA: VO

Aur apnay abbu ke khwaab ko bhulakar… mein poore jee jaan se jewelry store ko aur behtar banaane mein lag gayee…

Ek dinn Subhashini jee mere store per aayeen…

MIRA

Hello…

SUBHASHINI

Mira tum… tumhaare baare mein maine pada thaa… ye jewelery store?

MIRA

Mera hai…

SUBHASHINI

Aur tumhaari padhaayee…

MIRA

Mere abbu ka khwaab thaa ki mein padh-likh kar apnay pairon per khadee houun…

Look of Subhashini to Mira

Mein apnay pairon per khadee ho chuki hoon… issliye ab mein padhayee nahin karoongi… balki padhayee ke unn paison se unn ladkiyon kee madad karoongi jo ki zarooratmand hain…

Look of Subhashini to Mira

Kyunki mein nahin chahti ki koyee aur ladki mere jaisa kadam uthaaye…

Look of Subhashini to Mira
She pats her shoulder

SUBHASHINI

Mira mere khyaal se… tum kuch aur karo naa karo… padhaayee zaroor poori karo… kyunki tumhaare abbu ka pehla sapna yahee thaa ki tum padho-likho… aur tumhein apnay abbu ka khwaab zaroor poora karna chahiye… aakhir padhayee ke liye hee to tumnay itna bada kadam uthaaya thaa…

Look of Mira

SUBHASHINI

Ye meri sirf ek advice hai… issper amal karna tumhaara kaam hai… per meri baat per gaur zaroor karna…

Look of Mira

MIRA

Sure… aaiye mein aapko apna naya collection dikhaaoon…

Scene – 63

MIRA

Subhashini jee kee baat ne mujhe pareshaan kar diya thaa… ek taraf Raghav chahta thaa ki mein uska store sambhaaloon aur doosri taraf mere abbu ka khwaab thaa… mein karoon to kya karoon… mein isee pasho-pesh mein thee… ki ek dinn Brad mere paas aaya…

Dissolve to

Scene – 64

Visual: We pull out from Mira sitting with the lap-top on the bed, Brad comes to her

BRAD

Mira…

Mira looks at Brad

MIRA

Kya hua Brad baday down down lag rahay ho?

BRAD

Aaj… dad ka phone aaya thaa… tau kee dad se kaafi zor zor se baatein ho raheen theen…

MIRA

Kya? Per kyun?

BRAD

Tau ne store tumhein de diya hai naa…

Mira looks at Brad and slumps on a chair
Charge on Mira

Scene – 65

Visual: Mira comes to Raghav in his bedroom

MIRA

Raghav… tum ye store ke papers vaapas le lo…

Raghav looks at Mira with a question in his eyes

Mein nahin chahti ki iss store kee vajah se tumhaare aur Viki ke beech mein koyee ladayee ho…

RAGHAV

It's OK… ye sab mera kamaaya hua hai… jisay mein chaahoonga… usay mein doonga… issmein Viki ko ya phir tumhein koyee problem nahin honi chahiye…

MIRA

Per…

RAGHAV

Mein chahta hoon ki iss store ko vaapas vohee naam milay jo ki ek zamaane mein iska hua karta thaa… and I have concrete plans for it… dekho maine ek fashion show ke zariye store ko re-launch karne ka socha hai… lap-top mein plan ka blue print hai… aao dikhaata hoon…

Raghav takes Mira to the lap-top
Charge on Mira

Scene – 66

Visual: Shot of Jewelry store

MIRA: VO

Raghav ke plans ke mutaabik, humnay fashion show kee poori taiyaari kar lee thee…

Scene – 67

MIRA

Jiss dinn show thaa uss subah Viki Raghav se milnay aaya… Viki ne Raghav ko accuse kiya ki vo apnee saari daulat mujhper luta raha hai… unkee bahas iss hadh tak badhee kee Raghav ne Viki ko chaanta maar diya…

Gussay se ubalta Viki Brad ko lekar usee waqt vahan se chala gaya…

Scene – 68

Visual: Mira working at the store
Visual: Mira looking out for Raghav
Visual: Mira calls Raghav

MIRA: VO

Mein vaapas store aa gayee… fashion show kee taiyaari karvaane ke liye…

Fashion show shuru honay waala thaa per Raghav ka kuch bhi ata pata nahin thaa…

Maine Raghav ko call kiya…

MIRA

Raghav… kahan ho tum… tum abhi tak aaye kyun nahin?

RAGHAV

Ek baat boloon…

MIRA

Hmmm…

RAGHAV

Gussay mein tum ekdum TIGRESS ke jaisee lagtee ho… gussa chhodo aur show per dhyaan do… varna tumhein TIGRESS jaisee dekhkar, saare guests bhaag jaayengay…

MIRA

Ha ha… that's not funny…

RAGHAV

I will be there honey… don't worry…

Visual: Mira walking frantically

MIRA: VO

Fashion show shuru ho chukka thaa… per Raghav nahin aaya… maine usay call kiya… per usnay phone nahin uthaaya… meri intuition mujhe kisi anhonee ka ehsaas kara rahee thee…

Flashcuts: Fashion Show

Scene – 69

Visual: Mira comes in the bedroom… sees Raghav is lying on the bed dead…

MIRA

Mein fauran ghar pahunchee… aur ghar per mujhe Raghav kee laash mili…

Fade to black

Scene – 70

Exterior shot of Nirbhay's pad

Dissolve to

We dissolve to the nirbhay's flat floor
Mira is sobbing

NIRBHAY

MIRA… control…

Look of Mira
MIRA controlling her tears

NIRBHAY

Thanks for your story… tumhein insaaf dilaana ab media ka kaam hai…

Scene – 71

We pull out from a table. Coffee mugs are kept on it.

DINESH

To tum kehna chahte ho ki Mira nirdosh hai…

Nirbhay looks at DINESH... he says in a very serious tone...

NIRBHAY

Hmmm…

Look of DINESH

Believe me… pahle to mein uske ooper sirf story karna chahta thaa… per ab mujhe Raghav murder case ka expose bhi mil raha hai… We have TWO VERY BIG STORIES…

DINESH gives a long stare to Nirbhay

DINESH

SUNDAY… mujhe har haal mein dono stories Sunday tak chahiye…

NIRBHAY

Done …

Scene – 72

Montage cuts of Nirbhay
Montage cuts of various news offices

Scene – 73

Two plain clothed cops are watching television

FIRST COP

Pahle to sirf politicians hee thay… ab to iss media ne bhi naak mein dum kar diya hai… kitnay cases vaapas khulvaayengay… abhi Jessica Lal ka case thanda bhi nahin hua hai… aur ab ye case aa gaya…

Scene – 74

Visual: Dinesh Gautam is breaking the news

DINESH

Breaking news mein… VIRGIN MIRA naam se bahucharchit Mira Ali maamle mein adaalat ne aaj ek mahatvapoorna faisla diya… media kee sargarmi ke chalte… adaalat ne maamle mein pesh sabooton mein kayee khaamiyaan paayeen…

The voice overlaps as we dissolve to

Dissolve to

Scene – 75

We dissolve to a top angle shot of the top of the tree
We close on Mira sitting on a bench in the park… total seclusion… no one around… except for stray chirps of the birds…
We come to mira… she pulls out a cigarette from the pack… about to light it up… then suddenly she crushes the pack and throws it off…
We come to mira's face… her eyes are closed… fists are clenched… the expressions say as if she has been vindicated… she is heaving heavily…

DINESH GAUTAM: VO

Aur Mira ko baizzat baree kar diya gaya…

Gyaat ho ki media ne iss case se juday kayee pahluon ko ujaagar kiya thaa…

Jab Mira fashion show mein thee to vo Raghav ka murder kaise kar sakti hai…

Raghav ek strong built ka aadmi thaa… kya police ko lagta hai ki Mira jaisee ladki Raghav ko overpower karke usay maar saktee hai…

Raghav ke bhateejay Brad ke mutaabik… Viki ne Brad ko raaste mein hee ek motel mein chhod diya thaa… jahan se Brad ko uski maa niki ne pick kiya thaa… ye vohee waqt hai jiss waqt Raghav ka khoon hua… aakhir Viki uss waqt kahan thaa?

Aur ek dilchasp baat… Viki kee building ke watchman ke mutaabik… Viki jabse Raghav se milnay gaya thaa… tabse vo building mein vaapas nahin aaya hai… aakhir Viki hai kahan?

Adaalat ne police ko iss case per vaapas phir se kaaryavaahi karnay ke aadesh diye hain…

Dissolve to

Scene – 76

Visual: Dinesh Gautam is breaking the news

DINESH

Breaking news mein… VIRGIN MIRA naam se bahucharchit Mira Ali… Raghav Krishna hatyakaand se baizzat bari honay ke baad… apnee padhaayee ko jaari rakhnay ke liye US jaa raheen hain…

Cut of Brad watching the news

Dissolve to

Scene – 77

Visual: Mira is with Nirbhay…

NIRBHAY

Kya tum vaapas aaogi?

MIRA

Pata nahin… sabkuch mere course per depend karta hai… mere peechay se Subhashini jee store ko sambhaalengi… just see if you can help her out…

Nirbhay looks at Mira, smiles and nods
Just then they hear a loud overlap sound: **MIRA**
They turn and see, Brad running towards them

BRAD

Mira… tum mat jaao…

Look of Mira

MIRA

Jaana to mujhe padhega… mujhe padhaayee jo karni hai… apnay abbu ka sapna poora karna hai…

Look of Brad to Mira

BRAD

Mein jaanta hoon ki tum vaapas aaogi…

Look of Mira

MIRA

How can you say that?

BRAD

Gyaan… ladkiyon ka kaafi gyaan hai mujhe…

Brad looks at Mira and smiles
Mira looks at Brad, she sees a reflection of Raghav smiling in Brad's face
Mira kisses Brad on the cheek lightly, she gets up and walks off
Brad looks at Nirbhay
Nirbhay smiles
Brad too, smiles

BRAD

I LOVE HER…

NIRBHAY as he looks at Mira walking off

Even I love her…

Look of Brad to Nirbhay
Look of Nirbhay to Brad, Nirbhay closes his eyes

FADE TO BLACK

Credit titles roll by

EPILOGUE

Amit R Agarwal has always believed that today is the age of smart work.

Hard work is passé, smart work is the key for success.

Working smart, Agarwal has a very developed and established network worldwide, other than making his own films, he is helping others find success in the industry as well.

He helps with script-doctoring, gap-funding, sales and acquisitions of films.

Virgin.. Mira is already being developed in the International Market

The development of the film for the Indian market will be initated soon

Thanks for reading the book

The Making of Virgin.. Mira

Hope, if you are working in films, you find your journey easier!

Thank you.

Before I leave, I want to tell all the readers, how smart work gives you the power and position to help the future generation and the generation that will follow them to help realize their dreams!

My mother's dream was that I study at the Oxford University! One thing I couldn't achieve in my life.

I distinctly remember my Maa telling me, not to get disheartened. At the end of the day it is all about doing something in life. Do something, such that you can help people get to Oxford!

When you apply to the Oxford University or any of the top-Unis in the world, your application has to be supported by a credible reference, a professional from the field that can vouch for your skills and capability that you will complement the course or the subject-matter that you want to pursue and will be an asset for the university.

I am very happy that today applicants to the Oxford University approach yours truly to write a reference for them and the University of Oxford accepts them!

graduate.admissions@admin.ox.ac.uk   12:18 AM (12 hours ago)

to me

Dear Mr Agarwal ,

Thank you for submitting a reference for in support of their application to the Master of Fine Art (Full-time) at the University of Oxford, for entry in 2023/24

Your reference letter will now be added to 's application

and the University of Oxford are very grateful for your assistance in this admissions process

Yours sincerely,

Graduate Admissions

University of Oxford | Graduate Admissions and Recruitment
University Offices, Wellington Square, Oxford, OX1 2JD
Enquiries and questions: Graduate Admissions

UNIVERSITY OF OXFORD | Graduate Application Form

Reference Submitted

Your reference has been submitted.

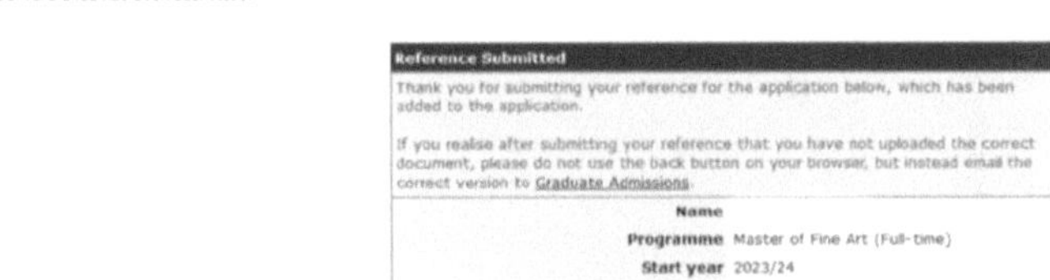

Reference Submitted

Thank you for submitting your reference for the application below, which has been added to the application.

If you realise after submitting your reference that you have not uploaded the correct document, please do not use the back button on your browser, but instead email the correct version to Graduate Admissions.

Name	
Programme	Master of Fine Art (Full-time)
Start year	2023/24
Application Reference ID	0-

I am elated that I can help this generation of students and future generations with their study plans at the University of Oxford.

I hope this book has motivated you all enough to conquer all odds and emerge winners in life.

www.ingramcontent.com/pod-product-compliance
Ingram Content Group UK Ltd.
Pitfield, Milton Keynes, MK11 3LW, UK
UKHW042019190726
13854UKWH00005B/2359